"Are you still [ ] date of yours?" J

Claire burst out laughing. "Are you kidding? It's strange, but I almost feel as though I've never even *talked* to a boy before!"

"Oh, come on," Jean teased, "After all, you've been on the football team, Claire! You *can't* feel uncomfortable around boys."

"Well, I don't know," Claire said doubtfully. "Dating a football player is a lot different from passing him the ball."

"You mean your date is a Gladiator?" Jean asked excitedly.

Claire nodded.

"What a coincidence! So is mine! And he's really good looking, too."

"Mine, too," Claire whispered.

Jean laughed. "I just can't get over the coincidences. They're both on the team. They're both really handsome. I'm almost afraid to ask what position he plays."

"Quarterback," Claire whispered.

"Quarterback?" Jean repeated. "But Scott Trost and Ken Matthews are the quarterbacks. And Ken goes out with Terri." Jean tried to remain calm. "Claire, *I'm* going out with Scott."

Claire blinked. "But that's impossible, Jean. *I'm* going out with Scott!"

Bantam Books in the Sweet Valley High series
Ask your bookseller for the books you have missed

THE DATING GAME

Written by
Kate William

Created by
FRANCINE PASCAL

BANTAM BOOKS
NEW YORK · TORONTO · LONDON · SYDNEY · AUCKLAND

RL 6, age 12 and up

THE DATING GAME
A Bantam Book / September 1991

ISBN 0-553-29187-4

Published simultaneously in the United States and Canada

Bantam Books are published by Bantam Books, a division of Bantam
Doubleday Dell Publishing Group, Inc. Its trademark, consisting of
the words "Bantam Books" and the portrayal of a rooster, is Registered
in U.S. Patent and Trademark Office and in other countries. Marca
Registrada. Bantam Books, 666 Fifth Avenue, New York, New York
10103.

PRINTED IN THE UNITED STATES OF AMERICA

OPM   0 9 8 7 6 5 4 3 2 1

One

Jessica Wakefield talked animatedly as she ate her lunch. "This is definitely going to be one of the biggest dances of the year," she said, her blue-green eyes sparkling with excitement. She looked from one friend to the next. "Not only is the gym going to be absolutely covered in paper flowers, but the dance committee got permission to use candles on the patio tables."

Sandra Bacon sighed. "Love in Bloom!" she exclaimed. "I think that's a great theme for a spring dance." She gave herself a hug. "And dancing by candlelight! Don't you think that's romantic?"

Lila Fowler, who had been examining her eyebrows in a compact, dragged her gaze away from her own reflection. Romance wasn't her top priority. "I only wish I could convince my father to buy me that gold bracelet I saw at Bibi's. I want to wear it to the dance," she grumbled. "I can't go to something this special in the same old jewelry."

Her friends exchanged a look among themselves. Bibi's was one of the most expensive boutiques in Sweet Valley, and Lila was one of the richest girls. *Poor Lila*, their looks said, *what a hardship.*

"Well, if I were you, Lila, I wouldn't care about going in the same old gold," said Amy Sutton. "I'd worry about having to go with one of the same old boys." She rolled her pretty gray eyes. "I think I've found the perfect date for you, Lila. There's this gorgeous new guy working in the record store at the mall. He's exactly the person you'd want to go to a romantic dance like this with. I even had a dream about him. But, of course, that doesn't mean I don't love Barry."

The other girls laughed. If they had a dollar for every boy Amy had ever dreamt about, they'd all be able to shop at Bibi's. And if they all didn't know that Amy was really and truly in love with her boyfriend, Barry Rork, they would have suspected Amy of scoping out the guy in the music store for herself and not Lila. Until Barry, Amy had had what they all had thought was a terminal case of the boy-crazies.

Only Jessica didn't join in her friends' laughter. Her mind was on something else. "Did anyone see that show about dreams last night?" she asked seriously. "It was all about analyzing and interpreting your dreams. It was really fascinating. You'd be amazed how significant dreams can be."

Amy picked up her fork. She did not look interested. "You mean all that boring psychological stuff?" She raised one eyebrow. "Like, if you

2

dream that the cat gets lost, it means you secretly wish your brother would run away from home?"

Lila went back to looking at herself in her mirror. "Dreams are just dreams. They don't mean anything." She gave herself a smile. "Every time I eat too much pepperoni pizza late at night, I dream that my car's been stolen."

"Oh, I don't know if it's that simple," said Jean West suddenly.

The others turned to her in surprise. She had been so quiet during the conversation about the big dance that they had almost forgotten she was there. "I saw part of that program, and it really convinced me of how important dreams can be." She smiled ruefully. "I only wish I had some dreams worth interpreting," she added.

"The only dreams that are important are the ones about cute guys who drive sports cars," Amy said with a giggle.

"Really, Amy," said Jessica, with a toss of her shoulder-length blond hair, "sometimes you can be so superficial. Almost every culture that has ever existed has recognized the significance of dreams."

Lila snapped her compact closed. "Well, you certainly seem to have become the expert all of a sudden," she said. "Since when are you so well informed on the subject?"

Jessica smiled knowingly. The idea of being an expert appealed to her. "Well, if you must know," she said airily, "I've been doing a lot of reading about dreams lately." In fact, Jessica had read one magazine article, but there was no reason for Lila to know that. "And," she continued, lowering her voice in a way that was guaranteed to catch the

3

attention of her friends, "I've been having this one completely amazing dream lately."

"I bet it has something to do with shopping," teased Lila.

"As a matter of fact," Jessica replied coldly, "it doesn't have *anything* to do with shopping."

"Come on, Jessica, tell us what it is," Jean urged. "The most memorable dream I've had lately was about turning up for a football game in my pajamas instead of my cheerleading outfit."

But Jessica liked to be coaxed. "You really want to hear about it?" she asked coyly.

"Of course we do," said Sandra.

"Am I in the dream?" Lila asked.

Jessica ignored her friend and cleared her throat theatrically. "Well," she began, "I'm walking along the beach. I'm wearing my two-piece pink bathing suit, the one with the little bows. Anyway, every few feet I pass another cute guy I know. There's Nicholas Morrow, and A. J. Morgan, and Danny Porter, and Scott Trost. . . ." She paused to make sure she had everyone's attention. "All of them want me to sit with them, but I just keep on walking. And then, all of a sudden, I'm on a different beach and there's no one around at all." By now, even Lila was listening to her every word. "Then, the next thing I know, it's raining. But there's nowhere to go for shelter. I start running. I run and run. And then I trip on something. I fall in the sand, and I'm lying there, getting soaking wet and thinking that I'm never going to get back home again, when I feel someone putting a blanket around me." She took a deep breath. "I turn to see who it is, and there's the most gorgeous boy I've ever seen!"

4

"Does he have dark hair?" asked Amy.

Jessica picked up her sandwich. "Well, actually, I'm not sure about that. It's storming so severely . . ."

"Then how do you know he's so gorgeous?" asked Lila.

Jessica looked exasperated. "It's a dream, Lila. Of course he's gorgeous."

"So what happens then?" asked Sandra.

Jessica shrugged. "Then I wake up."

"It's like real life," said Jean. She smiled. "Just when you get to the good part, it ends."

The other girls glanced at one another uneasily. Jessica knew that Jean, of course, was talking about herself and Tom McKay. They had really seemed to be made for each other, but then Tom had broken off the relationship, much to Jean's confusion and surprise.

Sandra touched her best friend's shoulder. "Don't worry, Jean," she said gently. "You'll find the right guy for you yet."

Jessica tapped on the table. "Hey," she said, "don't you want to hear what my dream means?"

"I know what it means," said Lila. "It means you should never walk on an empty beach without an umbrella."

"I've had it three times," Jessica went on. "Everybody knows that if you have the same dream three times, it means it's going to come true."

Amy laughed. "You mean you really are going to get caught in a storm on the beach?"

Jessica was too excited to be discouraged. "Of course not. The beach isn't what's important. It's the *boy* who's important." She looked from one to another of her friends triumphantly. "This boy is my one true love."

"*Your* one true love?" Sandra repeated.

"Yes," Jessica said firmly. "I just know that it's him."

"Maybe I'd better start dreaming harder," Jean said, laughing.

"Maybe you should, Jean," Jessica advised her solemnly. "Dreams do come true, you know."

Jessica's twin, Elizabeth Wakefield, was sitting on the opposite side of the cafeteria with her boy-friend, Todd Wilkins, her best friend, Enid Rollins, and Claire Middleton. Like her identical twin, Elizabeth was a classic California blond with blue-green eyes and a tiny dimple in her left cheek. The sisters looked so much alike that even their parents had trouble telling them apart. But that was where the similarities ended. For while Jessica's favorite pastimes were shopping, going to parties, and dating every good-looking boy she met, Elizabeth was a hard-working student and a serious young woman who preferred spending time with Todd or a few close friends to a hectic social scene.

She was far from serious now, however, as she teased Claire about the Love in Bloom dance that was less than two weeks away. "How about it, Claire?" Elizabeth said with a smile. "Who's the lucky guy going to be?"

Claire flushed. She hadn't been at Sweet Valley High very long, and although she'd made a name for herself by becoming the first girl in the school's history to try out for the Gladiators,

Sweet Valley High's football team, she hadn't yet dated anyone. "I'm not really much of a dancer," she said shyly.

"You don't have to be much of a dancer to go to a dance," Todd said. He gave Claire a mischievous grin. "Look at Elizabeth. She's got three left feet, but I can't keep her away from the dance floor."

Elizabeth punched Todd playfully in the arm. "Tell the truth," she laughed. "You're the one with the extra left feet!"

"Anyway," said Claire, "it doesn't matter how many left feet I have. I don't think anyone's going to ask me."

"Oh, come on," Enid said, "don't be modest, Claire. Any girl as intelligent, as nice, and as pretty as you are has to have her admirers."

"Not to mention any girl who's as good a quarterback as you are," Todd added.

"And don't tell me there isn't someone you're interested in," Elizabeth prompted. She smiled impishly. "Some handsome football player, maybe?"

Automatically, all four of them glanced over at the next table, where several of the Gladiators were noisily inhaling their lunches.

Claire's cheeks turned a bright pink. "Well," she whispered, "there is this one boy who seems pretty nice . . ."

"Does he wear a helmet and like to go into a huddle?" Enid asked teasingly.

But Claire shook her head. "I'm not telling. I don't want to jinx myself." She stood up and pushed in her chair. "Anyway," she said, "I've really got to get going. I've got this major English project to do. I want to go to the library before my next class to see what I can find."

"I'll come with you, Claire," said Enid. "I have to return a couple of books I borrowed."

Once they were alone, Elizabeth turned to Todd. "Claire's really nice, isn't she?" she asked.

Todd started to reply, but his words were drowned out by a sudden burst of hilarity from the next table.

They both looked over.

Tim Nelson was choking with laughter. "Oh, right, Trost," he gasped. "And who are you taking to the dance if you're so fussy?"

Scott Trost, the handsome quarterback, was sitting at one end of the table, looking smugly amused by Tim's question. Not long before, Scott had been temporarily suspended from the Gladiators because of poor grades, but now he was back on the team and playing even better than before. For all his good sportsmanship, Scott didn't mix much socially. Some people said this was because he was shy. Some said it was because he was stuck-up. "If I don't have a date for the dance," said Scott, sounding anything but shy, "it's because I don't want one."

The other boys started laughing again and pounding on the table with their hands.

"Oh, right," said Zack Johnson. He winked at his teammates. "That's not the way I hear it, Scott."

Scott raised one eyebrow. "Oh, yeah?"

"*Oh, yeah?*" Zack mimicked. "I hear you've been dumped so many times, you're afraid to ask anyone out."

Scott looked shocked. "Me?" he asked. "Me,

dumped? You must be falling on your head too much, Johnson. Scott Trost does not get dumped."

"Except by Amy Sutton," Elizabeth whispered to Todd.

"Amy dumps everybody sooner or later," Todd whispered back. "She doesn't count."

"If you don't get dumped," Tad Johnson, Zack's older brother, broke in, "it's only because there isn't a girl in the school who would go out with you on a bet anymore."

"Is that so, Blubber?" Scott asked, referring to Tad by the nickname he'd been given because of his enormous size. "Are you sure you're not confusing me with yourself?"

Danny Porter, the team's quiet but cute and well-liked wide receiver, rapped on the table. "Come on, you guys," he said good-naturedly. "You don't have to start insulting each other." Then he shook his head. "On the other hand, Scott," he said with a grin, "you have to admit that you've got a little bit of an attitude problem when it comes to girls."

"Look who's talking," Scott shot back. "I don't see them lining up for you, Porter. You probably can't even remember your last date. Whereas I," he went on, "I could go to that dance with any girl I wanted, just like that," he said, snapping his fingers.

This time Danny's disbelief was genuine. "You're too much, Trost, you know that?"

"OK," Tim said, loudly enough to cause several more heads to turn toward his table. "Prove how popular you are, Mr. Wonderful."

Scott got to his feet and shoved his books under

his arm. "Don't you worry," he replied angrily. "I'll be at the dance. And I won't be alone!"

Elizabeth stared after Scott as he strode from the cafeteria. "I don't believe him!" she exclaimed, turning back to Todd. "Did you hear him? He's so arrogant! No wonder no one wants to date him," she fumed. "It surprises me that no one's tried to murder him."

Todd grinned amiably. "I wouldn't get too upset about it, Liz," he said mildly. "Scott's really not such a bad guy."

Elizabeth stared at Todd as though he'd just acquired a second head. "Not such a bad guy?" she repeated. "What are you talking about? Did you hear him? He acts as if he's the best thing to happen to women since pantyhose."

"He just got a little carried away with himself, that's all," Todd said. "You know how guys are. They like to brag. It doesn't really mean anything."

Elizabeth's blue-green eyes were blazing. "Well, it means something to me," she said shortly. "It means Scott's a creep."

"You should have heard him, Mom," Elizabeth said to Mrs. Wakefield. She deepened her voice in an imitation of Scott Trost. "I can have any girl I want."

Mrs. Wakefield smiled understandingly. "At least Todd's not like that," she pointed out, "and that's what really matters."

Elizabeth had an easygoing nature, but there were some things she felt very strongly about, and this was one of them. "It's a matter of principle, Mom," she explained. "That sort of shallow behavior really gets to me."

Mrs. Wakefield patted her daughter's shoulder sympathetically. "I know you like to stand up for your principles," she told her daughter.

"You know what it reminds me of, Mom? It reminds me of the beauty pageant. It's exactly the same kind of attitude." Recently, when a beauty pageant had been held in the auditorium of Sweet Valley High, Elizabeth led a protest against it because she believed that the emphasis of all those contests was on looks rather than on character and intelligence. "It's as if he thinks we're not people at all. To hear Scott talk, you'd think there was a girl tree or something, and that all he had to do was just reach out and pick the one he wants."

At that moment Jessica drifted into the kitchen, a dreamy expression on her face. Catching the end of her sister's sentence, she came to an abrupt stop and widened her eyes. "So what's wrong with going after what you want?" she said.

"That's not what we were talking about," Elizabeth tried to explain. "We were talking about boys who think that any girl should be thrilled to get a date with them."

Jessica stared blankly at her twin. Elizabeth sighed. She knew Jessica seriously believed that any boy she liked should be thrilled to go out with her, so it was difficult for her to appreciate the point Elizabeth was trying to make. "I don't see what's wrong with a little self-confidence," she said at last.

Elizabeth turned to her mother for support, but Mrs. Wakefield had ducked behind the refrigera-

11

tor door. Elizabeth smiled inwardly. She knew that after a hard day at work, the last thing her mother wanted was to be caught in the middle of her opinionated twins. "Jessica," Elizabeth said in exasperation, "I'm not talking about self-confidence. I'm talking about egotism."

But Jessica still seemed distracted. "No, you're not," she said. "You're saying that a person who's in love shouldn't go after what she, or he, wants."

It was Elizabeth's turn to stare blankly at her sister. Sometimes it was hard for her to believe that they lived on the same planet, let alone that they were identical twins. "Jessica," said Elizabeth reasonably, "I didn't say anything like that. I'm talking about boys who—"

"I don't know about you, Elizabeth Wakefield," Jessica interrupted, "but I believe in true love. It's everyone's destiny. And everyone has a right to go out and find it, no matter what." With a toss of her head she marched from the kitchen.

Elizabeth turned back to her mother.

Mrs. Wakefield cautiously emerged from behind the refrigerator door. "Well," she sighed, "I wonder what brought on that little speech?"

Elizabeth shook her head. "I don't know," she said slowly. "But knowing Jessica, I'm sure it won't be long before we find out."

Later that evening, Elizabeth went into Jessica's room to patch things up. She was feeling a little bit upset about their argument. She knew that the scene in the cafeteria had put her in a bad mood.

Jessica was sitting on her bed, surrounded by

piles of books, papers, and clothes. Elizabeth carefully picked her way through the litter of Jessica's possessions that covered the floor. She made a little room for herself on the edge of the bed. "I just wanted to say I'm sorry about this afternoon."

Jessica didn't look up from her book. "Oh, that's OK," she said breezily. "I forgive you, Elizabeth."

Elizabeth smiled. "Gee, thanks, Jessica," she said sarcastically, "that's incredibly understanding of you."

"Love has made me understanding," Jessica replied.

Jessica had been in love more times than most people had had hot dinners, so Elizabeth decided to change the subject. "What's that you're reading?" she asked.

Jessica held up the book. On the cover was a photograph of clouds. "It's called *Understanding Your Dreams*," she explained, as though Elizabeth couldn't read the jacket herself. "And it's absolutely tremendous. You wouldn't believe all I've learned already."

Elizabeth frowned. "Don't you have a big project for English due soon?"

Jessica waved aside her sister's concern. "I've already done tons of work on that," she assured her. "Anyway, this book is much more interesting than making a mock travel brochure." Jessica grimaced. "I always thought travel was supposed to be so interesting, but it isn't when you have to *write* about it. It's unbelievably dull! Now, dreams," she continued enthusiastically, "are an entirely different story. I could read about them forever!"

Two

Jessica burst into the kitchen on Tuesday morning in a blaze of tropical colors. She was wearing a wildly patterned skirt in greens and blues and purples, a pink top, and several bright scarves.

Mr. Wakefield looked up from his breakfast in surprise. "Are you going to school or to a luau?" he asked with a smile.

Jessica was too excited to answer. She leaned against the back of her chair. "You'll never guess what happened to me last night!" she cried.

Mrs. Wakefield, accustomed to such announcements, continued buttering her toast.

"Um, let me think," Elizabeth said, pretending to be deep in thought. There were times when she couldn't help but tease her twin. She snapped her fingers. "I've got it! You fell asleep!"

But this morning, humor was lost on Jessica. *"Then* what, Liz?" Jessica asked eagerly. "What happened *after* I fell asleep?"

"You started to snore."

14

"Elizabeth," Jessica groaned, "I'm trying to be serious." She glanced around the table, her face glowing with excitement. "Give up?" she asked brightly. "OK, I'll tell you!" She paused for dramatic effect and then she made her announcement. "I had my dream again last night!"

Her family's response to this news was not overwhelming. Her mother took a bite of toast. Her sister poured herself some juice. Her father helped himself to cornflakes.

But Jessica was not easily discouraged. "Can you believe it?" she persisted. "It's the fourth time in a row!"

Mr. Wakefield turned to his wife. "Dream?" he asked.

Mrs. Wakefield nodded. "Jessica's been having the same dream for the past few nights," she explained.

"Four nights," Jessica corrected.

Mrs. Wakefield smiled. "Four nights," she amended. "She dreams she's on the beach."

"That's not a dream," said Mr. Wakefield. "Jessica usually *is* on the beach."

"Not this beach," Jessica corrected again. "Wait'll you hear all the details, Dad."

Elizabeth and Mrs. Wakefield glanced at each other. They had already heard the first three versions of Jessica's dream in some detail.

"I'm walking on the beach in my pink two-piece . . ." Jessica began.

And now it seemed that they were going to hear the fourth as well.

Elizabeth ate her cereal while Jessica babbled on. She wondered if her mother had also noticed that every time Jessica retold the dream it changed slightly. This time, the storm was a hurricane, Jessica was wearing a sarong, the sand was black, and there were a lot of large white flowers growing on the beach.

"Don't you see?" demanded Jessica. "It's Hawaii! The beach in my dream is in Hawaii!"

"Because you're wearing a sarong and the sand's black?" asked Elizabeth. "Jessica, there are beaches with black sand in New England. It doesn't mean—"

Jessica cut her off. "Not just because of the sand and the sarong. Because the guy in my dream is a surfer."

"Jessica," said Mr. Wakefield, "would you pass me the milk?"

"Dad! You're not paying attention. I'm right in the middle of my dream."

"And I'm right in the middle of my breakfast," said Mr. Wakefield, nodding at his cereal bowl.

"I feel this surfer's arm around me," Jessica continued.

"How do you know he's a surfer?" Elizabeth interrupted.

Jessica gave her sister a stern look. "I can just *tell* he's a surfer, Elizabeth. That's what happens in dreams." She turned to her father. "Anyway, I feel his arm around me but the storm's so bad that I can't really see him. I catch a glimpse of his shoulder, though!" She sat back, a look of triumph on her pretty face. "He's wearing a Hawaiian shirt!"

"Oh, I see," Elizabeth said solemnly. "A Hawaiian shirt. That's conclusive proof if ever I heard it."

"Excuse me, Jessica," said Mr. Wakefield. "But do you think I could have the milk now?"

Jessica, oblivious to her father's request, pointed a spoon at her sister. "You can laugh if you want, Elizabeth Wakefield. But I know that this boy is my one true love. And I know for a fact that he's waiting for me in Hawaii!"

Elizabeth glanced at her watch. It was almost time to go. "Jessica," she said patiently as she got to her feet, "you haven't even seen his face. He's a dream! How can you be in love with him?"

Jessica pointed the spoon again. "Love isn't about reason, Elizabeth," she explained. "Love is about destiny. It's not something you can control."

Elizabeth threw up her hands in surrender. "I give up!" She laughed. "There's no use trying to argue with you when you've made up your mind."

"That's right," said Jessica proudly. "There isn't."

Mr. Wakefield cleared his throat. "Jessica, do you think there's *any* chance I could have the milk now?"

Sandra Bacon steered her mother's Toyota into the school parking lot. "I just can't believe no one's asked you to the dance yet," she said to Jean West. "What's wrong with the boys in this school?"

Jean laughed. "They're all blind?" she suggested.

Holding her breath, Sandy squeezed the Toyota into a tight space. When there was no sound of metal scraping against metal, she turned off the engine and started to breathe again. She turned

17

to her friend. "I'm serious, Jean. You're pretty, you're popular, you've got a great personality . . ."

"I guess that's not what the guys are looking for this year," said Jean as she rolled up her window. "To tell you the truth, Sandy," she said slowly, "I really don't know if I'm ready to start dating again."

Sandy climbed out of the car and locked the door. "Because of what happened with Tom?" she asked.

Jean nodded. "I don't want to be hurt like that again," she said softly.

They started walking toward the school. "Jean," Sandy said gently. "I know how much you liked Tom, but don't you think it's time you gave somebody else a chance?" She put her arm around her friend's shoulders. "You're so terrific. It really upsets me to see you sitting home by yourself every Saturday night."

Jean smiled. "Well, if things keep up like this, I'm going to have to find a new hobby. I've already rearranged my closet fifteen times!"

Sandy laughed, but her eyes showed real concern. "It's just not right," she said. She turned her face toward the bright blue sky. "What a beautiful spring day!" She took a deep breath. "I have a feeling, Jean. Love is in the air!"

Jean took a deep breath. "That's not love," she said. "That's car-exhaust fumes."

Despite what she'd told Sandy, Jean found herself humming a happy song as she approached her locker. She had the sneaking suspicion that the word *love* appeared somewhere in this song.

18

Jean West, she told herself as she opened her locker, *you've got a touch of spring fever!* Jean put her math book on the shelf and took out her English notebook. *We're going to have to do something about this*, she told herself. *Spring fever can be a dangerous thing!* She bent down to put her sneakers on the floor of her locker. Then she stopped. There was something there. It was a lilac-colored envelope. *Someone must have put it in the wrong locker*, she thought. Jean picked it up. Her name was written across the envelope in an unfamiliar handwriting. She turned the envelope over several times. And then it came to her. *It must be an invitation! That's why it's on such fancy stationery.*

Jean pulled a single lilac sheet of paper from the envelope. It was not an invitation; it was a letter, written in a painstakingly neat hand. As Jean read it through, her expression changed from curiosity to surprise.

Dear Jean,

I've been trying to get up the courage to write you this letter for a long time. Sometimes when I pass you in the hall, I want to reach out and touch you. I want to say, "Hey, Jean, look at me. I'm looking at you." But you're such a special girl, I'm afraid you'd just laugh at me. I'm afraid you'd turn away and take my heart with you. I'm not a poet or anything, Jean, I'm a quarterback. I'm a good quarterback. But when it comes to telling a girl like you how I really feel about her, well, I guess I never really got off the bench. I could tell you that I think you're the most beautiful girl I've ever seen, but why should you believe me? I could tell you your skin reminds me of pearls and your

*eyes remind me of stars, but you've probably heard
that a billion times before. What if I told you that
whenever I hear you laugh my heart skips a beat?
What if I told you that I can't imagine anything
that would make me happier than to walk down
the hall with you beside me? No, that would be a
lie. What would make me happiest would be to
think that there was a chance that someday you
might feel for me just a little of what I feel for
you. If there's even the smallest chance that this
miracle might happen, put a note in my locker and
maybe we could make a date. If it turns out that
you feel nothing for me, my heart will be broken,
but I will understand.*

Yours hopefully, Scott Trost.

Jean stared at the signature in disbelief. Scott
Trost? Scott Trost had a crush on her? Scott
Superjock Trost wanted to go out with her? She
read the letter one more time. It sounded genuine. And anyway, who would be mean enough
to write a note like this as a joke?

A little shiver of excitement ran through her.
Scott Trost wanted to date her!

Although Jean had never really thought of Scott
as a boy she might be interested in, maybe she
should go out with him now that she was free.

After all, he was good-looking, and a hard-
working student. And he was one of Sweet Valley
High's top athletes. When she'd sat next to him
in history class one year he had seemed pleasant
enough. She had a vague recollection of him recit-
ing a funny poem about Paul Revere to her. That
meant he had a good sense of humor.

On the other hand, Scott Trost did have a reputation for being pretty arrogant. She'd heard him called "Mr. Macho" by a girl in her gym class who had dated him briefly. And Amy Sutton had dumped him pretty quickly. But, considering the fact that Amy had dumped him because he'd been suspended from the football team, her opinion couldn't be counted.

Jean became dimly aware that a bell was ringing. She looked around. The hall was empty. That must have been the last bell! Jean slammed her locker shut and raced off to class. *Scott Trost*, she thought to herself as she hurried along. *Scott Trost*. She slipped into the classroom and into her seat. *Maybe Sandy was right*, she told herself as she opened her notebook. *Maybe love really is in the air!*

Scott's unexpected attention had thrown Jean into confusion. It was true that she had never thought of Scott Trost as a possible boyfriend. But by the end of the day, she had more than made up for the lapse. Not only had she thought of nothing else, but she had brought his name into every conversation, hoping to find out a little more about him. Maria Santelli thought Scott was OK, but she really didn't know him well. She figured he was the sort of boy who hung out with other boys and didn't really have any female friends. Winston Egbert thought Scott took himself too seriously, but that he meant no harm. Ken Matthews thought he was an excellent quarterback. Tim Nelson couldn't get over the fact that Scott had restored his Corvette all by himself. Amy said Scott was an OK dancer but that he never talked about anything but himself. Lila didn't think Scott's parents were very well off, but she did grudgingly admit that the Corvette was a pretty nice car. "It always surprises me how much some people can do without money," she had said. Zack Johnson thought Scott bragged too much. Cara Walker thought he was pretty nice. Sandy thought he was cute, but too quiet. When Jean tried to discover just how many girls Scott had dated and dumped—or had been dumped by—she found out that he had gone out once or twice with a few different girls, but that the only serious girlfriend he'd had was Amy. Having Amy as a serious girlfriend, Jean knew, was like having lawn mowing as a serious career. When she left school, she was more confused than ever.

"Hey, Jean," Jessica called as Jean drifted by her. "What's up? You look like you're a million miles away."

Jean laughed self-consciously. "Oh, no," she said quickly. "I was just thinking about . . . um . . . my history homework."

"Ugh." Jessica frowned. "Don't mention home-work. I've got a big project for English. You want a lift into town?" she asked, holding up the keys to the Fiat she shared with her sister.

All day long, Jean had been thinking about going into town and getting a new lipstick and a batik scarf she had seen in the Blue Parrot. It would go well with her best white dress, and she wanted to look particularly nice the next day. "Where are you going?" she asked.

Jessica immediately became mysterious. "Oh," she said evasively, "I've got a few errands to run. I'll let you off by Caster's."

"Sure, I'll take a lift," Jean decided.

As she climbed into the Fiat, it occurred to Jean that she hadn't yet pumped Jessica for information on Scott. If there was any girl who knew more about the boys at Sweet Valley High than Jessica, Jean certainly hadn't met her.

But Jean's hopes for learning anything from Jessica were dashed immediately. No sooner had Jessica turned the key in the ignition than she started talking about herself. Or, to be more precise, about her dream.

"So then it starts pouring," Jessica was saying as the school disappeared behind them. "Not just rain, you understand, but a major hurricane. The palm trees practically touch the ground!" They stopped at a light. "Did I tell you that in the dream I'm wearing a purple sarong and a necklace of flowers?"

"No," Jean said. It had taken several minutes for Jessica to get from the first part of her dream to the second, and Jean was feeling a little numb.

Jessica nodded. "And I think I also have a pink flower in my hair."

The light changed and the Fiat moved ahead.

"And then I trip on something in the sand. I'm not sure if it's driftwood or the fin of a surfboard . . . "

Jean nodded absentmindedly.

"He has the most incredible smile," Jessica said enthusiastically.

"That's just the most amazing dream." Jean sighed. "And you really think this boy is the one?"

"Oh, I'm certain of it," Jessica replied confidently. "I've studied a lot about dreams, you know, and that's the way I interpret it."

Jean turned so that she was looking at Jessica's perfect profile. She knew that Jessica loved being

23

asked for advice, whether she had any to give or not. "I was wondering," she said slowly, "if you could give me a little help with a dream. I've had it twice and I just can't figure out what it means."

"Sure," Jessica said immediately. "Tell me all about it."

Jean began to recount the event of the morning as though she had dreamt it. "Well, I dreamt I found a note on the floor of my locker."

Jessica nodded. "Go on," she ordered.

Jean finished her story.

"So you have no idea who the boy is?" Jessica asked, frowning thoughtfully.

Jean laughed nervously. "When I'm asleep I know who it is, but when I wake up, I have no idea."

"Classic," said Jessica. "Absolutely classic. Then what happens?"

"Well, nothing happens," Jean answered lamely. "The letter is full of stuff about how much he cares about me, and how he doesn't want me to break his heart . . ."

Jessica sighed. "It's almost as romantic as my dream!"

Jean took a deep breath. "The thing is, Jessica," she said, "that even in the dream I'm really confused about this boy. I don't know what it is about him, but even though I'm happy to have gotten his letter, I'm not quite sure how to react."

They came to a sudden stop in front of Caster's. Jessica drummed on the steering wheel thoughtfully. "It seems to me you're not sure if this dream means you're about to fall in love, or if it's a warning that you should be careful you don't make the same mistake you made with Tom."

24

Jean felt herself blushing. Jessica knew even more about love and boys than she had thought. And Jessica certainly seemed to know more about Jean herself than she'd given her credit for. "Well . . . um . . . yeah," she stammered. "I guess maybe it is something like that."

"OK," Jessica said. "I'll tell you exactly what the dream means." She looked Jean in the eye. "You see, the paper the letter is written on is very important. The fact that it's fancy means that this love letter is very serious. This guy really cares."

"You really think so?"

"Absolutely." Jessica leaned closer to Jean. "The problem is that he's not confident enough to admit it."

Jean thought about this for a minute. The one thing no one had said about Scott was that he was too insecure. "You think so?"

Jessica nodded. "Yes, I do." She put her hand on Jean's. "Jean," she said solemnly, "when love knocks, you've got to open the door."

Jean got out of the car and watched Jessica steer the Fiat back into traffic. Jessica's words echoed through her mind. "When love knocks, you've got to open the door." She would do it, she decided. She would open the door and let love in. With a new assuredness, Jean headed toward the card store, wondering whether she should buy blue notepaper or pink.

Elizabeth and Jessica had had another argument before dinner. It was Jessica's night to fix dinner, but she had gone straight to the library after school and had not come home until late.

"Well, what's more important?" Jessica had demanded. "Who makes the spaghetti sauce, or that my homework gets done?"

"Some people can do both," Elizabeth retorted.

By the time she was ready to go to bed, Elizabeth was feeling a little guilty about having been so hard on her sister. After all, Jessica did seem to have a lot of homework. She had come home with half a dozen library books! After she had brushed her teeth, Elizabeth walked through the bathroom to Jessica's room to say goodnight.

Will wonders never cease? Elizabeth thought. Jessica Wakefield, the girl who was born to shop and party, was sitting at her desk, surrounded by a stack of books.

"Wow, you really are working hard on that English project," Elizabeth exclaimed.

Jessica looked up. "What did I tell you?" she asked. "You're not the only one who knows how to study."

Elizabeth made her way to the desk. "So," she said, "how's it going?"

"If you don't mind, Elizabeth," Jessica said coolly, "I'm trying to get some work done here. I can't have all these interruptions. If you've come to say goodnight, then say goodnight and let me get on with it."

"Well, excuse me, Jessica Einstein. I was just trying to show a little interest."

Jessica bent her head over her book. "I don't need your interest, Elizabeth," she said stiffly. "I need peace and quiet."

Before Jessica could stop her, Elizabeth leaned over and picked up one of the library books. She stared at the title for a second in puzzlement. *Your*

Dreams and You. She looked at the others. *The Key to Your Dreams. Your Dreams: What's in Them for You? Hawaii: Island Paradise. The Visitor's Guide to Hawaii.*

Jessica wasn't working on her English project at all! She was working on her dream!

"Jessica Wakefield," Elizabeth said, sounding very much like the older sister—even if she was only four minutes older. "I can't believe you're doing this when you have more important things to do!"

"More important?" asked Jessica. "What's wrong with you, Liz? What could be more important than love?"

Elizabeth closed her eyes. Was there any person on the entire planet more exasperating than her sister? No, she decided immediately, there wasn't. One minute she wanted to date every cute boy in Southern California, and the next she was making speeches about the importance of true love.

"As far as *you're* concerned," said Elizabeth sternly, "passing English is more important than love." She put her hands on her hips. "Unless you're planning to spend the rest of your life as a high-school junior, that is."

"Don't be ridiculous," Jessica snapped back. "I'm planning to spend the rest of my life in Hawaii."

Three

Elizabeth had a dream, too. In Elizabeth's dream, there was an enormous tree growing right in the middle of the Sweet Valley High lawn. She knew as soon as she saw it that it was an apple tree, even though there were no apples growing on it. What was growing on it were girls—hundreds of girls, each wearing a bathing suit with a sash across her chest, as though she were in a beauty pageant. The girls were smiling. Standing around the tree was a large crowd of boys. Scott Trost was their leader. He pointed up at one of the girls in the tree. "I'll take that one," he said. The girl he pointed to started to climb down the tree. But then Scott snapped his fingers. "Wait a minute!" he ordered. "I've changed my mind. I don't like the color of her bathing suit. I'll take that one over there instead."

The dream was so vivid that when she came down to breakfast on Wednesday morning, Elizabeth could still see Scott Trost and hear his fingers snapping. She thumped down the stairs and into the kitchen. *Where does he get off, treating people like objects?* she fumed to herself. *Whatever happened to love and respect? The nerve of him! The arrogance! I'd like to put Scott Trost in a tree and leave him there for the rest of the year!*

Mr. Wakefield looked up as his older daughter marched into the room, her pretty face scowling, her lips moving. He glanced over at his wife.

"Is there something wrong, Elizabeth?" Mrs. Wakefield asked as Elizabeth threw herself into her chair.

Elizabeth looked at her parents as though she hadn't realized they were in the room. "Wrong?"

"You seemed to be talking to yourself," Mr. Wakefield pointed out. He smiled. "Now, I know that I sing in the shower, but on the whole we Wakefields don't usually talk to ourselves unless there's something wrong."

Elizabeth laughed. "No," she said with a shake of her head. "Nothing's wrong. I was just thinking." She helped herself to some juice. "About relationships. You know, between men and women."

"Oh, relationships between men and women," said her father. His voice was serious but there was a twinkle in his eye. "No wonder you were talking to yourself."

"Is this because of what happened at school the other day?" asked Mrs. Wakefield.

Elizabeth nodded. "It's got me wondering what people really look for in relationships. Do you think most boys just want someone pretty who will tell them how wonderful they are all the time?"

Mrs. Wakefield frowned thoughtfully. "I think it's unwise to make generalizations, Elizabeth," she replied. "But on the whole, I think most people, whether they're male or female, want a friend and companion, a *real* person. Don't you think so, Ned?"

Mr. Wakefield winked. "Not me." He grinned. "*I* was looking for a pretty woman who would tell me how wonderful I was all the time." He touched his wife's arm. "But then I fell in love with your mother. I had to settle for a real person instead."

"Oh, you." Mrs. Wakefield laughed and squeezed his hand affectionately.

The three of them were still laughing when Jessica rushed into the kitchen. "You're not going to believe this," she said dramatically. "You're just not going to believe this!"

Elizabeth looked up at her sister. Jessica's eyes were sparkling and her cheeks were as bright as the tropical-flower earrings that dangled from her ears. To match the earrings, she was wearing a hot-pink sundress. Elizabeth smiled. Ever since Jessica had decided that her dream man was waiting for her in Hawaii, she'd been dressing in anything she owned that was at all tropical. *We're lucky she doesn't own a grass skirt*, Elizabeth thought as she surveyed her sister's outfit.

"Please, Jessica," Mr. Wakefield begged. "Tell us! I can't stand the suspense."

"Jackson!" announced Jessica.

Her family looked at one another and then at Jessica.

"Isn't that incredible?" Jessica squealed. "His

name is Jackson!" She hugged herself. "Isn't that the most romantic name you've ever heard?"

Mr. Wakefield seemed a little lost. "I thought Jackson was the name of a town," he said.

Elizabeth was skeptical. "How did you find out his name?"

Jessica collapsed in her seat. "He's so gorgeous." She sighed, ignoring her sister's question. "You just wouldn't *believe* how gorgeous he is."

"I thought you said you couldn't see his face," Elizabeth said.

Jessica picked up the box of cornflakes. "I saw him last night when he told me his name," she said.

Mr. Wakefield shook his head. "This is all beyond me," he confessed. "I'm going to work. Understanding the law is a lot easier than understanding Jessica and her life."

Elizabeth stood up, too. "I want to get to school a little early to see if I can catch Penny Ayala," she explained. "I want to talk to her about an idea I've got for an article in *The Oracle*."

No sooner had Elizabeth and Mr. Wakefield gone than Jessica turned to her mother with one of her brightest smiles.

"Mom," Jessica began, fidgeting with excitement. "Mom, if I raised enough money for the fare, would you let me go to Hawaii by myself?"

Mrs. Wakefield looked fondly at her younger daughter. She knew from experience that Jessica's enthusiasm probably wouldn't last long enough for her to raise enough for a bottle of sun block. "Of course, dear," she said. "That seems perfectly reasonable to me."

Jessica leapt from her chair and threw her arms around her mother. "Oh, thanks, Mom," she shrieked. "You're the best mother in the world." She hugged her again. "And don't worry, Mom," Jessica reassured her. "I'll send you a postcard as soon as I arrive."

Jean usually drove to school with Sandy, but that morning she had made up an excuse and taken an early bus instead. She wanted to slip her note into Scott's locker before anyone else was around.

Her heart pounding, Jean walked down the hallway. She hadn't felt this happy in ages, not since things had been good with Tom. It was the letter from Scott that had made her realize how really down she'd been. Her breakup with Tom had been a big blow to her self-confidence. Just the thought that someone was interested in her again had changed her outlook overnight.

Feeling like the heroine in a romantic spy movie, Jean slipped the pale pink envelope into Scott's locker. The note she had written simply said that she'd very much like to get together, and she had put her phone number on the bottom. Jean stood there staring at the battered metal door, imagining the note drifting toward her destiny. She heard voices behind her and gave herself a shake. *This is no big deal*, she told herself. *At the most, I'll probably have one boring date with the guy*. Filled with resolve, Jean turned on her heel.

She'd only gone a few steps when she saw Scott coming toward her. Her heart gave a leap and her new-found calm dissolved into a frenzy of indecision.

Scott was with Ken Matthews, and the two of them were laughing. She'd never realized Scott had such a warm laugh. Jean wondered if she should say hello. If she didn't say hello, he might think she didn't like him. If he hadn't seen her, her suddenly saying hello might embarrass him. But she was standing right by his locker. She knew that he must have seen her. Slowly but surely, Jean started down the hall. Maybe the best thing to do would be to pretend that she hadn't seen them, she thought. But how could she pretend that she hadn't seen them? They were both over six feet tall. They weren't that easy to ignore. Jean approached the two boys. The boys approached her. Jean took a deep breath. They were almost abreast of each other. Scott was smiling. His smile was as warm as his laugh. Jean got ready to nod. Suddenly, Scott turned his head away. Her face burning, Jean hurried past. *It's nothing personal*, she told herself. *It doesn't mean he's changed his mind. He's probably just shy*.

Scott was shy at lunch as well. Shy, but extremely cute. He was sitting at the Gladiators' table with Ken and Winston Egbert and Danny Porter. A lot of their meal involved loud laughter and throwing wads of paper and bits of food at one another. But it did not involve Scott glancing her way, not even accidentally. For all her good intentions, Jean couldn't stop herself from looking over at him whenever she could.

"I know you agree with me, don't you, Jean?" Jessica's· voice, which Jean had only been

33

vaguely aware of, suddenly brought her back to her own table with a start. "Huh?" Jean said.

Scott might not be paying her any attention, but her friends were all staring at her curiously.

"Oh, sure," she said quickly. She had no idea what they had been talking about. "Of course I agree."

Jessica turned to Lila. "You see?" she said. "At least Jean appreciates the importance of dreams."

Lila stabbed a slice of cucumber. "You've convinced me that dreams are important, Jessica," she said patiently. "But I still think you're crazy to turn down a date with Steven Anderson just because of some guy in a dream." She waved her fork in Jessica's direction. "Really, Jessica. Steve Anderson is not only mega-handsome, he drives an MG Midget."

Jessica tossed back her hair. "I wouldn't care if he drove a Jaguar," she said airily. "All I care about is getting to Maui."

Cara shook the last potato chip out of a bag. "Isn't there an old saying about one hunk in Sweet Valley being worth two in Hawaii?"

Jessica noisily pushed her chair back and stood up. "I'm really disappointed in you," she told her friends. "Except for Jean, not one of you has a romantic bone in her entire body."

"I think an article on what attracts boys and girls to each other is a terrific idea," Enid said to Elizabeth. She broke a cookie in half. "I'm not surprised Penny went for it in a big way."

Elizabeth gave her friend a pleased smile. "The best part is that it isn't going to take as much time to do all the research as I thought." She nodded to her left. "Claire came up with the brilliant idea of doing a questionnaire."

At the sound of her name, Claire, who had been staring absentmindedly at the next table, turned to Elizabeth with a vague smile.

"I'd like *everyone* to answer it," Elizabeth explained, "but I'm really interested in getting replies from the kids who are actually in couples."

"Well, you can count me out. As usual," Enid said with a short laugh. She and her last boyfriend, Hugh Grayson, had broken up a while previously because he didn't live in Sweet Valley and it was hard for them to find time to be together.

"You'll meet someone soon," Elizabeth said brightly. "And I was also thinking that it might be nice if Claire took a photograph of one of the couples to go along with the article." Elizabeth turned to her friend. "Claire, what do you think?"

Elizabeth followed Claire's gaze and found herself looking at the back of Scott Trost's head. Surely Claire couldn't be interested in Scott Trost. Only a few minutes before, Claire had been telling her she thought sensitivity was the most important quality a boy could have. Elizabeth shifted her gaze slightly so she was looking right into the smiling face of Danny Porter. Elizabeth sighed with relief. *That* made sense.

Claire picked up her sandwich and turned to Elizabeth as though she'd been paying attention all along. "That sounds great to me, too," she said. A sudden smile lit up her face. "Hey, I have an even better idea, Elizabeth. Why don't I photograph you and Todd?"

"Perfect!" Enid grinned. "Sweet Valley's Couple of the Year!"

"To go or not to go," Jean mumbled to herself as she left her last class. She was torn between hurrying home so she'd be there when Scott called, and hanging around school on the chance that they might bump into each other. In the end, she decided to make a quick detour past his locker on her way home. If they ran into each other, it might save him the price of a phone call.

But instead of seeing Scott, Jean bumped into Claire Middleton. Claire was standing by Danny Porter's locker, the one next to Scott's. She looked as surprised to see Jean as Jean was to see her.

"Hi, Claire," Jean said.

Although she and Claire didn't know each other well, they both worked at Project Youth once a week, helping out in the after-school program for the children of working parents. They had had a few friendly conversations, and had discovered that they both really enjoyed the work.

"I was just on my way home," Jean explained unnecessarily.

"Oh, me, too," said Claire quickly.

Jean smiled. Claire shifted nervously from one foot to the other. Neither of them seemed to be able to think of anything else to say.

"Well . . ." Jean began.

"Say, you haven't seen Scott Trost around, by any chance?" Claire asked suddenly.

"Scott?" Jean repeated. She now understood what it felt like to be tackled.

"Yeah," Claire said. Then she added quickly,

"He borrowed my Spanish notes and I need them back to study for a quiz."

Jean began to breathe normally again. "Oh, your Spanish notes." She wondered if Claire noticed her relief. "No, I haven't seen him since lunch. I mean, I didn't really see him at lunch. I just noticed he was around."

Claire shrugged. "Oh, well," she said lightly. "If you see him, would you tell him I was looking for him?"

"Sure," said Jean. "Sure, I'll do that."

"Well, bye," said Claire.

"Bye."

As soon as Claire had disappeared, Jean hurried out of the building, across the lawn, and to the bus stop. On the ride home, she glanced at her watch at least every forty-five seconds. She couldn't stand the slowness of the bus and got off a stop early to run the rest of the way home. She flew through the front door and came to an abrupt stop in the living room. Something was wrong. Jean held her breath and listened. The house was silent. The telephone wasn't ringing. She went to the answering machine and saw that the red light was blinking. Scott must have called before she got home.

Jean dumped her books on a chair and pushed the playback button. There was a message for her father from her Uncle Bill. There was a message for her mother from the dentist's office. There was a message for Jean from her mother saying she'd be a little late getting home.

Oh, well, Jean told herself brightly. *It's a little unrealistic to think he'd have called already.* She looked at her watch again. It was five minutes later than it had been the last time she had looked. It was really much too early to expect a call, Jean realized. In fact, he probably had practice that afternoon. She went into the kitchen to get herself a snack. She checked her watch against the kitchen clock. No, it was definitely much too early.

By six o'clock, Scott still hadn't called. Jean decided that he must have stopped at the Dairi Burger after practice with some of the guys from the team.

At seven o'clock, she began to worry that he hadn't gotten her note. Maybe there was so much junk at the bottom of his locker that it had gotten lost.

At eight o'clock, Jean decided that she must have put the note in the wrong locker. She figured she had put her note in Danny Porter's locker. Right at that moment, Danny was probably telling every other boy on the team that she had sent Scott a note on fancy pink stationery, asking him to call her. She groaned, imagining how they would tease Scott mercilessly and convincing herself he would never go out with her now.

At nine o'clock, Jean realized that she had put the note in the right locker, but that Scott had decided the whole thing was a mistake.

At ten o'clock, Jean went to her room. She put on her headset and lay on her bed in the dark. She didn't know her mother was calling her until the light suddenly went on.

"Jean!" Mrs. West said loudly. "Jean! What are you doing in the dark? Didn't you hear me? There's a phone call for you!"

38

It was probably Sandy, Jean thought. She always called for a chat around this time, after she'd finished her homework. Jean picked up the phone in the upstairs hallway. "Hi," she said, trying to sound a little more cheery than she felt.

"Hello? Jean?"

It wasn't Sandy.

"Jean?" the voice repeated.

It was Scott. She couldn't seem to speak. She stared at the phone as though it had suddenly changed into a small reptile with buggy yellow eyes.

"Jean?" She could hear him slapping the receiver in the palm of his hand. "Jean, is there something wrong with this connection? Do you want me to call you back?"

With an enormous effort, she located her voice. "Scott," she said, miraculously sounding normal. "Hi."

He definitely had the nicest laugh she had ever heard.

"At last," he said. "I was beginning to think that you were trying to put me off."

"Oh, no," said Jean quickly. She may have found her voice, but she could hardly hear it above the pounding of her heart. "I haven't changed my mind."

"Then how about Saturday night?" he asked. "I thought we could meet at the Box Tree Café at eight. If that's OK with you?"

"That's OK with me," said Jean.

Four

"Well?" Jessica demanded. "What do you think?"

Elizabeth had gotten up early on Thursday morning to check over her questionnaire one more time before she brought it into school to be copied and distributed. Normally, this would have meant that she had at least a half-hour of peace and quiet, because Jessica never got up one minute sooner than was absolutely necessary. Jessica's idea of being early for something was not being late.

Elizabeth turned at the sound of her sister's voice. Not only was Jessica awake, she was dressed and waving a light blue sheet of paper for her sister to see.

"What is that?" asked Elizabeth. From where she was sitting, she could just make out the heading: *Dreams Unlimited*. Elizabeth experienced a familiar sinking sensation. *Now what's Jessica up to?* she wondered.

"I had fifty copies made at Copy-Rite yesterday afternoon," Jessica explained. "I was going to show them to you last night when I got home from Lila's, but you were already asleep!"

Elizabeth smiled to herself. Leave it to Jessica to act as though her sister should apologize for going to bed!

Jessica crossed the room and proudly put the paper on the desk in front of her twin. "Doesn't it look great?" she asked excitedly. She leaned over her sister's shoulder and read out loud. " 'Dreams Unlimited. Understand your dreams. Discover your destiny. Unlock the secrets of love. Expert analysis and interpretation of your dreams. Confidential.' " At the bottom of the page was Jessica's name and phone number.

Elizabeth looked from the flyer to her twin's beaming face. *Expert?* she repeated to herself. *Confidential?* Didn't Jessica realize she could be arrested for false advertising?

"So?" Jessica prompted. "Don't you think it's terrific? It solves all my problems. Don't you think it's the best idea I've ever had?"

Considering some of the ideas Jessica had had over the years, Elizabeth thought, this might very well be the best—if only she could figure out what it was. "Well," she said slowly, "I'm not really sure that I understand—"

"Really, Elizabeth. Are you always so slow in the morning?" Jessica demanded impatiently. "This is how I'll be able to earn enough money to go to Maui and meet Jackson!" she explained.

"Um, Jessica," Elizabeth said, carefully choosing her words, "do you really think people are going to *pay* you to interpret their dreams?"

41

"Of course they will," Jessica replied. "Why shouldn't they? I'm an expert."

Elizabeth shook her head. There was one thing you could say about Jessica: she never underestimated herself. "You don't think 'expert' might be a slight exaggeration?" she asked gently. "I mean, you've really only been interested in dreams for a couple of days."

"I've been interested in dreams for almost a whole week," Jessica corrected her.

"OK," Elizabeth said. "But I'm not sure that qualifies you as an expert."

Jessica snatched the paper from the desk. "You don't think I can do it, do you?" she snapped. "That's what you're saying, isn't it, Elizabeth?"

Elizabeth sighed. "Jessica, that's not what I said at all. I only meant—"

But Jessica was already across the room. "I should have known I couldn't count on you!" she said hotly. Then she added dramatically, "But just wait, Elizabeth Wakefield. This time next year, you'll be visiting me in Maui!"

Jean was having one of those days. She had wanted to look especially nice just in case she bumped into Scott. This meant that she had had to try on six different outfits, three pairs of shoes, and redo her hair four times that morning. By the time Jean had felt confident enough to leave the house, she had missed her ride with Sandy, which made her late for history class. Mr. Fellows had looked up as she tried to slip quietly into the room. "Well, Ms. West," he had said, "how nice of you to decide to join us." The entire class had laughed. Then Jean had realized she had left her homework at home. And to top everything off, when she had passed Scott in the hallway on her way to her second class, he had done no more than nod at her. It had taken her over an hour to get dressed, and he had barely looked at her. She might as well have been wearing a plastic bag, for all he seemed to care!

Jean headed toward the cafeteria. The night before, they had talked for over half an hour on the telephone. Scott had sounded relaxed and interested. He had made her laugh. He had sounded sincere when he told her how happy her note had made him. And today he was ignoring her again. Was he trying to drive her crazy?

Jean frowned. The worst thing was that she couldn't really talk to anyone about him. At least, not while he was acting so oddly. The less everyone knew, the better. She didn't want everyone to feel sorry for her if it all went wrong.

Jean turned the corner, and there, right outside the cafeteria, tacking a flyer to the bulletin board, was the answer to her prayers.

"Jessica!" cried Jean. "You're just the person I was looking for!"

Jessica stepped back to look at her handiwork. "What do you think?" she asked.

Jean studied Jessica's Dreams Unlimited announcement. "It looks very professional," she decided.

Jessica tilted her head first to the left and then to the right. "Yes," she agreed. "You're right. It does look very professional, doesn't it?" She turned to Jean with a happy smile. "Everybody's really excited about it. Even Lila was impressed when I told her how pleased you were with my interpretation of your dream.''

"That's exactly why I was looking for you," Jean said quickly.

"You've had another dream!" Jessica's eyes were sparkling. "You've had another dream and you want *me* to analyze it for you!"

Jean grinned. "Exactly!"

Jessica put her arm around Jean. "For you," she said brightly, "the service is free!"

As they waited on the lunch line, Jean told Jessica her dream. She told her that she had dreamt that the boy who sent her the love letter had asked her out. It was obvious that he really liked her. "But then I'm walking down this sort of tunnel," Jean continued, "and I see him coming toward me."

"Who is he?" asked Jessica. "Is he good-looking? Do I know him?"

"You don't know him," Jean said quickly. "I don't know him." It amazed her how good she was getting at fibbing. "But he *is* good-looking," she added.

"I bet he's not as good-looking as Jackson," Jessica commented.

But Jean was not about to be sidetracked. "Anyway," she went on, "I think he's going to stop and talk to me. All my friends are with me, and I want them to see how much he really likes me."

Jessica put a plate of salad on her tray. "Am I in the dream?"

Jean nodded emphatically. "Oh, absolutely, Jessica. You're right beside me."

Jessica absorbed this information. "Go on."

"Well, that's exactly what happens," said Jean.

"He goes on. He doesn't say hello. He doesn't stop to talk. He doesn't even smile."

Jessica considered the information, then asked, "Is he alone or is he with his friends?"

Jean had a moment of panic. *Was he alone or was he with his friends?* She couldn't very well tell Jessica that sometimes he was and sometimes he wasn't. "He's with his friends," she ventured. From the look in Jessica's eyes, Jean knew she'd said the right thing. "They're all laughing and joking," she added in a sudden burst of inspiration.

Jessica picked up her tray. "This one's really easy to figure out, Jean," she said as they started to walk to the table at which their friends were sitting. "For a professional like myself, that is," she explained. "You see, this fits in perfectly with the first dream. In that one, he slipped the note into your locker anonymously. In this one, you know who he is and you know that he likes you, but when there are other people around, he's too shy to admit it."

At the table, Lila, Cara, and Amy were having an intense conversation about what they were going to wear to the dance. Jessica put her tray down.

"What this dream is telling you," she continued, "is that this guy is very sensitive and shy. I'd even guess that the fact his friends are laughing in the dream means he's trying to protect you. He knows you've been hurt before and he doesn't want to go too fast."

Jean couldn't help but smile. *Well, of course. That's it! It makes total sense. Particularly when you consider Scott's reputation and the ragging he takes from the other boys!*

Jean was so happy that she dropped her tray down on the table and gave Jessica an impulsive hug. "Jessica!" she fairly shouted. "Jessica, you are a genius! You are the best dream interpreter in the world!"

Everyone at the nearby tables turned to look at them. Even Lila suddenly stopped in the middle of a dissertation about shantung silk. Cara and Amy looked up in surprise.

All eyes on her, Jessica tossed her head and smiled.

"I really appreciate your helping me with this," Elizabeth said to Claire. The two girls were distributing Elizabeth's questionnaire during lunch period.

"Oh, don't mention it," said Claire. "I really do think it's interesting, you know. I can't wait to read your article."

"Well, will you look at that!" Elizabeth exclaimed. There on the wall was one of her sister's flyers. "Jessica Wakefield," Elizabeth said to the announcement, "you never cease to amaze me!"

Claire laughed. "I've been seeing them all over the school."

Elizabeth shook her head. "My sister and her crazy schemes." Her voice was full of affection as well as exasperation.

"Oh, I don't know how crazy it is," Claire said. She looked at Elizabeth shyly. "Promise you won't laugh?"

Elizabeth nodded. "Of course I won't laugh," she promised.

A faint flush colored Claire's cheeks. "Well, I was almost thinking of going to Jessica myself."

Elizabeth managed not to laugh, but she couldn't hide the amazement in her voice. "You? But Claire, you're so practical and down-to-earth!"

Claire's blush deepened. "Well, it's just that I had a dream and it's been driving me nuts."

"What's it about?"

Claire took a deep breath. "I'm on the football field. It must be during a game, but I don't really see any crowd, and at first I'm the only player on the field. I'm running toward the nine-yard line with the ball under my arm. And then, all of a sudden, I see one of my teammates off to the right, waiting for me to pass the ball. Then I look to the left, and there's another Gladiator waiting for me to pass the ball to *him*."

"Do you know who they are?" asked Elizabeth.

Claire shook her head. "No. They're wearing their helmets and for some reason I can't see their numbers. Anyway, I'm too busy to pay much attention to them, because right behind me, breathing down my neck, is Matt Ambers." Claire shivered and Elizabeth understood why. Matt Ambers was Big Mesa's star tackle. If she had been in Claire's shoes, she wouldn't want him after her, even in a dream. "The thing is," Claire said, "I wake up before I can decide which player I'm going to pass the ball to." She laughed self-consciously. "I usually don't think twice about my dreams, but last night was the *second* night I had it, and for some reason it's really bothering me." She laughed again. "I guess it's so weird because I'm usually very good at making split-second decisions."

47

Elizabeth smiled. "Um, Claire," she said gently, "you don't think that this dream might be similar to something that's going on in real life, do you?"

"Like what?"

Elizabeth shrugged. "Well, like maybe two boys have asked you to the dance?"

"Talk about dreaming," Claire answered good-naturedly. "Not even *one* boy has asked me to the dance!" Suddenly, she became more serious. "To tell you the truth," she said softly, "there *are* two boys who have been showing a little interest in me lately."

Elizabeth smiled. "I thought there might be."

Claire's cheeks turned bright pink. "Well, actually, one's interested in me, and I'm sort of interested in the other."

Elizabeth had a fairly good idea who was interested in Claire. She'd seen John Pfeifer, one of *The Oracle*'s staff photographers, hanging around Claire, offering to give her special help with her own work for the photography club. But who was the boy Claire had her eye on? Elizabeth didn't feel that she knew Claire well enough to ask. "Well," she said, "that's pretty similar to the situation in your dream. Maybe you aren't sure which guy you really like."

Before Claire could answer, they were interrupted by Danny Porter.

"Hi, girls," Danny said with a big smile.

"Hi," Elizabeth answered.

Claire mumbled something that sounded vaguely like a greeting and turned pink again.

Well, this is interesting, Elizabeth thought.

Danny started to talk quickly, as though he'd

48

been rehearsing what he was going to say and wanted to say it before he forgot his lines. "I don't know if it's all right, because I'm not part of a couple or anything," he explained, "but I was wondering if I could have one of your questionnaires." Although he was talking to Elizabeth, his eyes were on Claire.

Claire's eyes were on her shoes.

"Of course it's all right," said Elizabeth. "I want as many people as possible to fill one out."

"Great! I think it's a pretty fascinating idea," Danny said. He couldn't have been smiling any more broadly if Claire had a camera in her hands.

There were times when Elizabeth realized just how much she was like her sister, and this was one of them. She was sure she saw a budding romance here. What else could all this smiling and blushing mean? Instead of minding her own business, as she knew she should, she decided to push things along. "That's just what Claire was saying," commented Elizabeth.

It seemed to be just the push that Claire needed. She looked up at Danny and thrust a questionnaire into his hands. "Oh, it is," she said quickly. "It's really fascinating."

Elizabeth hid a smile. She had a pretty good idea of to whom Claire was going to pass the ball.

Every Thursday after school, Jean helped out at Project Youth. Usually, though, she didn't get there by walking on air. Today, however, Jean was definitely several feet above the ground as she entered the building.

Since her talk with Jessica, she was even more

49

excited about her date with Scott than she had been before. She couldn't wait to get to know him better. Jean smiled at her reflection in the glass of a display case.

"Well, you're looking very happy today," Claire said as Jean floated into the room where they worked.

"Well, I have a pretty special date this weekend."

"That's great!" Claire said.

Jean knew she could end their conversation right there, but for some reason she found herself saying, "The only thing is, it's been so long since I've been on a date, I'm not sure I remember how to act."

Claire brushed a strand of hair from her eyes. "I know what you mean," she said with feeling. "I've just been asked out for the first time since I've been at Sweet Valley, and I'm a little nervous myself."

"Really?" Jean couldn't believe her ears. Several of her friends, such as Sandy and Cara and Amy, had steady boyfriends. The others, such as Lila and Jessica, dated a lot. She had been thinking that she was the only girl in the entire school, if not the world, who hadn't had a date for ages, and here was Claire in the same boat.

Claire laughed. "I almost said no, just to avoid all the stress."

"Tell me about it." Jean grinned. "My date isn't until Saturday, and I've already changed my mind at least a dozen times about what I'm going to wear."

"Me, too!" Claire exclaimed. "My date's tomorrow, and I *still* haven't decided what I'll wear.

We're not going anywhere fancy, but I don't want to look too casual."

"On the other hand," said Jean, "you don't want to look too formal. You know, in case you suddenly decide to go bowling or something."

"What I worry about most are my knees," Claire confided. "If I decide to wear a dress, my knobby knees are going to show." She made a face. "But whenever I wear a *long* skirt I wind up tripping all over myself."

"With me it's my hair," said Jean. "It'll go frizzy for no reason at all. You can't imagine what a nightmare it is. Sometimes I think I should carry a paper bag with me, just in case."

Claire laughed. "I'll tell you one thing, I feel a whole lot better knowing I'm not the only one who goes through this sort of thing."

"So do I," Jean agreed. "Hey, I've got an idea. Why don't we go shopping together after school tomorrow?"

"You mean so we can sort of boost each other's morale?"

"Exactly," said Jean. "I can help you pick out an outfit for your date, and you can help me." She looked at Claire hopefully. "You know, it might help us both get over the first-date jitters."

Claire extended her hand for a shake. "You've got yourself a deal."

Elizabeth was ecstatic. Her questionnaires had only come out that afternoon, and already she'd gotten over a dozen replies. Now she needed to design a chart for assessing her results.

But just as she had begun, Jessica flung herself through the bathroom door and landed on Elizabeth's bed with a sigh.

Elizabeth looked over her shoulder. "Don't tell me you're finally off the phone," she said. Jessica had been on the telephone for most of the evening, interpreting dreams.

"I'm exhausted," said Jessica. "I'm absolutely exhausted. It's not easy being a professional dream consultant, Elizabeth. Believe me."

"Oh, I believe you," Elizabeth assured her.

Jessica sat up straight. "Do you think I'd look even more expert if I started wearing glasses?"

Elizabeth rolled her eyes. "What I think is that you're pretty lucky you don't have any schoolwork to interfere with your career."

"Elizabeth," Jessica replied, with all the patience she possessed, "I don't think you understand. Getting to Maui to save Jackson from a life of loneliness is a lot more important than a few trivial school assignments."

"Oh, of course," her sister agreed. "Does this mean you're already making a fortune with your new business?" Elizabeth asked.

Jessica examined some imperfection in her nail polish. "Well, not exactly," she finally admitted. "But if you knew anything about the business world, Elizabeth, you'd understand that it's too early to expect a profit. First I have to build up my reputation, and then I'll be able to start charging."

"In other words, you're not making any money."

Jessica got up and walked over to her sister. "It's only a matter of time." She picked up one of the questionnaires.

"Jessica," Elizabeth said, "does the word *Tofu-*

Glo mean anything to you?" One of Jessica's money-making schemes had involved selling Tofu-Glo, a natural beauty product, door-to-door. In the end, it had cost her money to get rid of the stuff. At the time, she had promised never to try another get-rich-quick scheme.

"Of course it does," Jessica said with a sweet smile. "It reminds me that I'll have to do something about my hair before I leave for Hawaii."

Five

" 'Which of the following is most important in a potential date?' " Jessica read out loud. " 'Looks, personality, character, popularity, other.' " While Elizabeth drove them to school in the Fiat, Jessica was filling out one of her sister's questionnaires. She made a mark with her pen. "Well, that one's easy," she said happily. "Looks."

"You can't be serious, Jessica," Elizabeth said sharply.

Jessica frowned. "Well, I guess clothes count a lot, too. I wouldn't want to go out with someone who dressed poorly. But you didn't list that answer, Liz."

Elizabeth turned into the school parking lot without saying another word. She didn't want to get into an argument with her sister this morning.

Elizabeth was locking the car when she heard a scream. It was Lila Fowler, hurrying across the parking lot, calling to Jessica.

"Jessica!" she shrieked. "Jessica!"

Elizabeth couldn't remember ever seeing Lila so excited. Had someone named a shopping mall after her, Elizabeth wondered.

Lila ran past Elizabeth without a glance, and threw her arms around Jessica as though she were a long-lost friend. "I take back every doubt I ever had about your dream business," Lila gushed. "You are absolutely out of this world!"

Elizabeth raised her eyebrows in astonishment. It was highly unusual for Lila to praise anyone who wasn't either rich, famous, or Lila Fowler. And she had a hard time believing that Jessica actually knew as much as she claimed about interpreting dreams.

"I told you I knew what I was doing, Lila," Jessica responded in a bored tone of voice.

"I'll say you do." Lila smiled an enormous smile.

Jessica couldn't maintain her pose of indifference for long. "What happened?" she asked with her usual enthusiasm. "Don't tell me your father bought you that bracelet?"

Lila held out her arm. Around her wrist was a new gold bangle. "Just as you predicted!" She slipped her other arm through Jessica's. "And that's not all! Remember what you told Amy about her dream about me at a party?"

Jessica nodded. "The one where you're all alone on the dance floor except for the band?"

"Well, you were absolutely right! It was just like you said. You told me I'd get involved with a musician, and guess what happened?"

Elizabeth winced. She had never before noticed how incredibly shrill Lila's voice could be when she was excited.

"What?" breathed Jessica.

"Amy introduced me to that dreamy guitarist who works in the music store in the mall and he asked me out!"

Arm in arm, the two friends hurried toward the school. Elizabeth stood by the car, watching them go. "Well, so long!" she called softly to their disappearing backs. "So long, Elizabeth," she answered herself. "See you later!"

"I'm not saying there isn't a lot of good information here," Todd said. He and Elizabeth were sitting together in the cafeteria, discussing her article for *The Oracle*. It was a discussion that was becoming a little heated. "All I'm saying is that maybe you're so convinced of what the results are going to be that you're not looking at the whole thing clearly."

"In other words," Elizabeth said, "you think I'm biased."

Todd shook his head. "I wouldn't say biased, exactly. I just think you're overlooking one little thing."

Elizabeth turned to him expectantly. "Really, Todd? And what would that be?"

"That sometimes boys act one way when they're with other boys, and another way when they're with girls."

"Meaning what?"

"Meaning that scene with Scott and the Gladiators the other day. Boys put a lot of pressure on one another to act tough and manly. I don't think Scott would have acted like such a jerk if the others hadn't been teasing him."

Elizabeth removed a piece of paper from her notebook. "And what about this?" she asked him. "This is the chart I've made of the answers I've received so far. Just take a look at it, Todd."

Elizabeth had divided the answers into those from males and those from females. Todd had to admit that from the responses she had gathered so far, it didn't look too good for the boys. Most of the girls had listed a combination of qualities they looked for in a date. But the majority of boys had listed looks as their first priority.

Elizabeth peered over his shoulder. "Now what do you have to say for your sex?"

"The thing is, Elizabeth," Todd reasoned, "we have no way of knowing if these guys were alone when they filled out the questionnaire. I mean, just imagine that you're Scott Trost or somebody like that, and you're sitting with a bunch of the other football players, and you're reading the questions out loud. Do you think any of them are going to say, 'Hey, I really dig girls who speak three languages and do volunteer work'?"

Elizabeth held back a smile. "I don't know why you can't just face the truth, Todd," she replied. "Boys are shallower than girls, and that's all there is to it. They're much more interested in looks than in brains or personality."

Todd looked offended. "Hey, what about me?"

She gave him a peck on the cheek. "You're the exception that proves the rule."

"Elizabeth, even *you* are interested in looks." Now it was her turn to look offended. Todd gave her a teasing nudge. "Come on," he prodded, "be honest. I know I'm an extraordinarily wonderful person, but I don't kid myself. If I had two green

57

heads and hair growing between my toes, I don't think you would ever have agreed to go out with me."

"Of course I would have." Elizabeth laughed. "Beauty and the Beast has always been my favorite fairy tale!"

The bus that Friday afternoon was slow and crowded. The trouble with public transportation, Jean told herself as they crawled along toward the mall, was that it wasn't private. All day long she had been looking forward to getting together with Claire and being able to talk about her date with Scott. She had imagined sharing her feelings over Scott's phone call. She'd even brought his letter with her, so she could read the more romantic bits out loud. She was also eager to hear about Claire's date. Knowing that someone else was experiencing the same agonizing feelings was very comforting. But here they were, forced to keep their voices low and to talk about school because everything they said could be overheard by the other passengers on the bus.

As soon as they arrived at the mall, however, Jean brought up the subject of their dates. "So," she said as they walked into Bibi's, "are you still feeling nervous about this date of yours?"

Claire burst out laughing. "Are you kidding?" She grinned. "Does the Dairi Burger sell hamburgers? It's so strange," she said, "but I almost feel as though I've never even *talked* to a boy before!"

Jean stopped to look through a rack of blouses. "Oh, come on," she teased, "it can't be that bad.

58

After all, you've played on the football team, Claire! You *can't* feel uncomfortable around boys."

"Well, I don't know," Claire said doubtfully. "Dating a football player is a lot different from passing him the ball."

Jean's hand froze in midair. "You're kidding!" she cried excitedly. "You mean your date is a Gladiator?"

Claire nodded.

"What a coincidence!" Jean laughed. "So is mine!"

Claire smiled back, looking both proud and shy. "To tell the truth," she said softly, "the guy I'm going out with is one of the Gladiators' best players."

"This is incredible!" Jean exclaimed. "So is mine. And he's really good-looking, too," she added in a soft voice.

"Mine, too," Claire whispered. She held a pale yellow blouse up to her and studied the effect in the mirror. "In fact," she continued, "if you want to know the truth, I'm a little surprised that he asked me out at all. I'm not really his type." She put the yellow blouse back on the rack and picked out a green blouse. "He usually goes out with girls who are more obviously feminine. You know, girls who are really pretty and sophisticated, like you." She smiled wryly. "Not every guy wants to go out with a girl who can outrun him."

Jean laughed. "I just can't get over the coincidences. They're both on the team. They're both really handsome . . ." She nodded her approval of the green blouse. "I'm almost afraid to ask what position he plays."

"Quarterback," said Claire immediately, still studying the green blouse critically.

"Quarterback?" Jean repeated. She looked at Claire, but Claire's eyes were on her own reflection in the mirror. "But Scott Trost and Ken Matthews are the Gladiators' quarterbacks."

Claire nodded absentmindedly. "You know," she said, "I think you're right. I think I like this one."

"And Ken goes out with Terri Adams."

"It's not too casual and it's not too formal. We're meeting at the coffee shop, but we might go on to a movie or something. This should be perfect."

"Ken and Terri haven't broken up, have they?" Jean asked.

Claire, still oblivious to the panic that was beginning to build in Jean's voice, shook her head. "Not that I've heard," she said simply.

Jean stepped between Claire and the mirror. "Claire," she said, trying to remain calm, "I don't think you're paying attention. The boy I'm seeing is a quarterback, too."

Claire blinked. "But that's impossible, Jean. The only quarterback besides Ken is Scott, and *I'm* going out with him."

Jean wasn't sure whether she wanted to laugh or cry. "Well, in that case, maybe we could save him some money and all go out together," she suggested with a short, dry laugh.

The full meaning of what Jean was saying suddenly hit Claire like a squad of linemen. "Wait a minute," she said. "You mean to tell me that *you're* going out with Scott Trost?"

"That's right." Surely this was some sort of mistake, Jean told herself. Maybe the date with Claire had been arranged long before hers had been. She swallowed hard. "He wrote me this incredibly romantic letter—"

"And he left it in your locker," Claire finished.

Jean's heart dropped to her feet. "How did you know that?" Suddenly, she understood everything. "That's why you were standing by his locker the other day!"

Claire nodded. "Did he tell you that your skin glowed like pearls and that every time he passed you in the hall, he wanted to reach out and touch you?"

Jean's feelings of confusion were rapidly being replaced by fury. "Yes!" she cried. "That's exactly what he wrote!"

Jean dug through her bag. "I just happen to have his letter with me . . ."

Claire opened her purse and started rummaging through it as well. "I think I've still got my letter, too," she said.

Jean handed her letter to Claire, and Claire handed hers to Jean. Standing side by side between blouses and sportswear, each read the other's love letter.

"That creep!" Jean said in a low but furious voice. "He's written the exact same letter to us both! Word for word!"

"I don't believe this!" Claire whispered. "They're identical!" She looked up, her eyes blazing. "Just wait until I get my hands on him, that two-timing cheat!" She shook her fist in the air. "And if you want to know the truth," she hissed, "he isn't even that great a quarterback, either."

Jean was speechless with rage. Well, she had wanted to know who would be mean enough to write a love letter as a joke, and now she knew! She reread Claire's letter, looking for something, anything, different about it. But except for Claire's name written at the top, it was the very same letter Scott had written to her. Scott had only been playing a game with them. As angry as she was with Scott, however, Jean was even more furious with herself. What a fool she'd been! The first boy to ask her out since her breakup with Tom McKay, and she'd been carrying on as though he were Romeo and she were Juliet. The thought of her behavior made her cheeks burn.

"Well," Claire said, "are you coming with me or not?"

"Where?" Jean asked, still stunned.

"To give Mr. Scott 'God's Gift to Women' Trost a piece of our minds."

Jean was about to say that of course she'd go with Claire when something occurred to her. They could go to Scott's house, yell at him, and then go home as though nothing had happened. But in school on Monday, Scott would tell his version of the story to all his friends. Everyone would be laughing at *them*, not at *him*. The scene was so vivid in Jean's mind that she could almost hear the entire football team laughing their heads off. *Jean West thought Scott Trost really liked her. What a riot!* "Wait a minute, Claire," Jean said. "I've got a better idea."

"What could be better than punching him in the nose?" Claire asked.

"*Really* getting even," Jean explained. "Showing him that *three* can play at this game."

62

Claire began to look interested. "And how would we do that?"

"We go along with his little charade and see how far he's planning to take it." She smiled. "After all," she reasoned, "we have the advantage of surprise. Scott wouldn't have tried this if he'd thought we'd find out about each other."

"And, let's not forget that there's strength in numbers," Claire pointed out.

Jean reached out and shook Claire's hand. "Trust me. We'll make Scott Trost wish he'd never learned to write."

"Whew!" Claire laughed with relief. "I'm sure glad that's over. It's not easy exchanging small talk with someone you'd like to run over with a tank." Claire had just gotten home from her date with Scott and had phoned Jean immediately.

"So what did he say when he saw me?" Jean asked. As part of their plan, Jean had been waiting inside the coffee shop, reading a book at a table near the door, when Scott and Claire walked in. At the sight of her, Scott had suddenly grabbed Claire by the elbow and marched her back out the door. Everything had gone as planned, except for an unexpected stab of jealousy Jean had felt when she noticed what a nice couple Claire and Scott made.

Claire laughed loudly. "Oh, it was so funny." She chortled. "Before we went in, he gave me this big buildup about how quiet and cozy the coffee shop was, but the second he saw you, he suddenly decided that it was too crowded and noisy! 'But, Scott,' I said, 'there's hardly anybody here.'

'No, no,' he said, 'I know a pizza place in Cedar Springs.' Can you imagine? Driving an hour to get a pizza?''

"So what was it like?" Jean asked.

"The pizza was OK. Not as good as Guido's, though, if you ask me," Claire replied.

Jean had been sitting by the phone all night, waiting for this call, and now Claire was talking about pizza! "Not the food, Claire," Jean said patiently. "The *date*."

She could almost hear Claire shrug.

"Oh, I guess it was all right. I'll tell you one thing, I'm really glad I didn't buy that blouse! What a waste of money that would've been."

"I wonder what my date with him tomorrow night is going to be like," Jean mused.

"Well, if mine was anything to go by," said Claire, "I'd take a book along, just in case."

Six

Mrs. West looked up at the clock on the mantel. "Don't you have a date tonight, honey?" she asked Jean. "It's already after seven."

Jean, still in the jeans and shirt she had been wearing all day, was sprawled on the couch, reading. "There's plenty of time," she said dismissively. "I'm not meeting him until eight."

Jean understood the puzzled look on her mother's face. Normally, if Jean was meeting a date at eight o'clock, she would have been locked in the bathroom since five o'clock.

Jean had decided that if Scott Trost wanted to treat her and Claire as if they were dolls and not real people, then she was going to act like a doll. A wooden doll. She wouldn't laugh at his jokes. She wouldn't be impressed by his tales of football glory. She wouldn't even admire his car. He could stand on his head for all she cared. She wouldn't respond.

Jean smiled at her mother. "I've never looked

forward to a date the way I'm looking forward to this one," she said truthfully.

Jean had never before been late for a date, but when she arrived at the Box Tree Café, Scott was already standing outside the restaurant. She spotted him from a block away. He was wearing a lightweight white suit with a pale blue shirt and a dark blue tie. She had never seen him dressed up before, and the effect was rather startling. He looked great.

Jean had wanted to annoy Scott by being late. But instead of looking annoyed, he was gazing around him with a lost-little-boy expression, and occasionally he glanced nervously at his watch. Could it be he thought she might stand him up? *Stop this right now, Jean*, she admonished herself. *This boy is a rat, not a human being. Don't start thinking anything good about him.*

When Scott finally noticed her coming toward him, his face lit up in such a way that Jean almost forgot her own advice.

"Jean!" he called. He laughed as she came up to him. "I was beginning to worry that something might have happened to you." His tone was light, but there was something serious in his eyes.

There was something serious in his letter, too, Jean reminded herself. "No," she said flatly. She was not going to apologize or make an excuse. "No, nothing happened."

But if he noticed that she was being less than friendly, he ignored it. "Well, that's good." He grinned. "I wouldn't want anything to happen to you."

Oh, sure, she told herself, *I bet you wouldn't! What would you do to amuse yourself in your spare time if anything happened to me?*

She smiled back. "Wasn't that Claire Middleton I saw you with in the coffee shop last night?" she asked brightly. "You left so quickly, I didn't have a chance to say hello."

Scott's jaw dropped open and he stared at her blankly. "Why, yes," he said finally, searching for words. "Yes, it was. We're . . . um . . . we're working on this Spanish project together . . ."

"Oh, really?" Jean said.

With an apparent effort Scott recovered the full use of his facial muscles. "Well," he said, "should we go inside?" For a moment he didn't seem to know what to do with his hands. He tried to take Jean's, then to put his arm around her waist. Finally, when she strode right past him, he stuck them in his pockets.

Jean occupied herself with reading the menu by the door while they waited to be shown to their table.

"You know, Jean," Scott said to the side of her head, "I'm really glad you could make it tonight." He leaned closer, so that his lips were almost brushing her hair. "Really."

It's incredible, absolutely incredible. How can he tell such lies and sound so sincere at the same time? Be cool, Jean, she advised herself. *This is not a person, this is an ego with feet.*

Jean spun around so quickly, she nearly whacked him in the face. "I've very glad I could come, too," she said sweetly. "That was really some letter you wrote."

It might have been the light in the restaurant,

but Jean could have sworn that when she mentioned his letter, he actually blushed. "Let's not talk about my letter, OK?" He laughed uneasily. "Let's just have a good time."

As the evening wore on, Jean had to admit that there were moments when, in spite of herself, she *was* having a good time. At school, Scott was all football hero, larger than life and brashly confident. He was always part of a crowd of laughing, rowdy boys. But that night he was quiet and thoughtful and disarmingly straightforward. In fact, she decided, this Scott was the same Scott who had talked to her on the phone the other night. He was funny. He was kind. He was interesting and interested in what she had to say. Though she was still angry with him, there were times when she found herself being charmed. Even though she knew what a double-crossing, self-centered creep Scott really was, there were moments when she found herself liking him. *Get a grip on yourself*, Jean ordered herself. *This is all an act. He's only pretending to be nice to you so he can make you look like a fool.*

"Do you remember when you used to sit next to me in history class?" Scott asked her after they'd ordered.

"It's practically the only thing I do remember." Jean laughed, completely forgetting that she had promised herself not to laugh all evening. "All those names and dates!" She shuddered in horror.

"What are you talking about?" he asked. "You were terrific in that class."

"Oh, I'm not so sure about that," she said quickly. "But what about football? You're a terrific quarterback."

He shrugged. "I'm not a natural, like Ken Matthews. I have to work at it." He gave her a smile that lit up their cozy corner. "But I really love the game, you know? I really do. That's why I was so upset when the coach suspended me from the team because of my grades." He shook his head. "I thought the world had come to an end. And then Amy . . . well, I was really down for a while."

"Oh, Scott," Jean said, "you shouldn't be so hard on yourself—" She stopped abruptly. *Oh no you don't, Jean West. Don't start feeling sympathetic toward him.*

"I don't mean to be too personal," he said gently, "but I figured you'd understand how I felt after Amy and I broke up because of what happened with you and Tom."

Jean was stunned by Scott's words. It had never occurred to her that he had given her and Tom any thought at all. If she didn't know how two-faced and insincere he was, she would have been really touched. "I . . . uh . . ." she stammered.

Scott reached across the table and put his hand on hers. "Look, I'm sorry, Jean, really. I didn't mean to upset you. It's just that I used to see the two of you together, and you seemed so close, and then afterward . . ." Noticing that she was staring at his hand as though it were something unpleasant, he pulled it away. "I just thought you seemed hurt, that's all," he mumbled. Then he gave her a wink. "If you want, I'll recite that funny poem, 'The Afternoon Walk of Paul Revere' for you again. It's the only thing I *do* remember from history class."

It was a warm and starry night. On the way

home, they played Name That Tune. One of them would hum a song, and then the other would try to guess its title. But because Scott was tone-deaf, every song he hummed sounded exactly like the one before. By the time they turned onto Jean's street, they were both laughing uncontrollably.

"You've got to give me your solemn word that you won't tell anybody about this," he begged. "My career as a rock star will be over before it's even begun."

"You could always go into hog calling," Jean said, grinning.

The Corvette came to a stop in front of her house. Scott shut off the engine and turned to her. "I just want you to know that I had a really terrific evening," Scott said with a smile.

The moonlight gave the interior of the car a dreamlike quality. Sitting there with Scott, it was almost impossible to believe that he wasn't really the sincere and honest person he seemed to be.

Scott rested his arm along the back of her seat and moved toward her. His eyes were on hers. "Jean," he said softly, moving a little closer. "Jean, I just want you to know that everything I said in that letter . . . I mean, it was a stupid letter, really, but everything I said in it was true." She could feel his breath on her cheek. "I mean," he whispered, "about how much I've always liked you and everything."

Yes, Jean thought, *it's almost impossible to believe that he isn't the sincere and honest person he seems. But not quite impossible. What a creep! Doesn't he have any sense of shame?*

The spell was broken. Jean was out of the car

and on the sidewalk so quickly that Scott found himself sprawled across her empty seat.

"Well, thanks for a very nice evening," Jean said politely. She gave him one of her brightest smiles. "Please don't get up," she said sweetly. "I can see myself to the door."

Later that night, Jean was on the phone telling Claire all about her date with Scott. "We met at the restaurant, and then we had dinner, and then he drove me home." She yawned. "Of course, he talked about himself most of the time. You wouldn't believe how forgettable it was."

"Oh yes I would." Claire chuckled. "At least you did better in the conversation department than I did." She laughed again. "Once we'd exhausted the topics of Spanish class and the Gladiators' chances next season, we didn't have much to say. I can't decide which amazes me more—what a bore Scott is, or what a liar."

Jean wound the cord around her finger. "Claire," she said slowly, "do you think he's going to ask you out again?"

Claire sounded shocked. "What are you talking about, Jean?" she demanded. "I thought that after your date we were going to have it out with him. I spent the entire evening practicing my 'Scott, you're a toad' speech!"

In her mind, Jean could hear Scott's voice, low and gentle, telling her how much he really liked her. Suddenly, the nice memories vanished. *That creep! How could he have toyed with me like that?* Being suspended from the Gladiators for the rest of his life wouldn't be punishment enough. Jean didn't want to confront him now. She wanted revenge.

"Oh, no, Claire," she said quickly. "It's too soon. We can't let him get off this easily."

Claire hesitated. "Well, I don't know," she began slowly. "You see, the thing is, there's this other boy I like a lot, and I think he's going to ask me to the dance."

"Claire, please," Jean pleaded. "You're the first girl in the history of Sweet Valley High to try out for an all-male team. You're a role model for us all. You *can't* let Scott Trost get away with treating girls like objects."

In the silence, Jean could feel her friend weakening.

"Look, Claire, I have a plan," Jean continued, "let's tell our friends all about our wonderful dates. The news will be all over the school by lunch on Monday. Then when we confront him, we'll have an audience!"

Claire sighed. "It's just that I really like this other guy, Jean."

"Claire, this isn't going to mess anything up for you." She paused for a second to gather her thoughts. "Claire, you wouldn't want to miss seeing the expression on Scott's face when we show him up in front of the entire school, would you?"

"No, I guess I wouldn't." Claire laughed. "After all," she added, "it's true what they say, isn't it? A picture is worth a thousand words!"

*　　*　　*

Mr. Wakefield walked into the living room, a puzzled expression on his face.

Mrs. Wakefield glanced up from the book she was reading. "Something wrong, Ned?" she asked.

Mr. Wakefield lowered himself into his favorite chair. "No. It's just that on my way downstairs, I saw Jessica in her room. It's Saturday night. Jessica hasn't been home on a Saturday night since she discovered dating."

"I know it's hard to believe." Mrs. Wakefield smiled.

"She was sitting at her desk, surrounded by books."

"I guess Jessica's finally becoming responsible," Mrs. Wakefield said. "Isn't that nice?"

Mrs. Wakefield was right. Jessica *had* become responsible. She'd become responsible for the dream life of half of the girls in the junior class. She couldn't believe it herself. Here it was, Saturday night, and instead of being out having a good time, she was slaving away at her interpretations. Not, of course, that she wanted to be out having a good time. Not when the only boy in the entire world who interested her was waiting in Hawaii for her arrival.

Jessica looked up from her work with a sigh. "Boy," she said out loud, "I had no idea so many people spent so much time dreaming. When do they find the time to do anything else?"

She got up from her desk and collapsed on her bed. Surely she had proven herself talented enough by now to expect some payment for all her hard work. If she didn't start making some money soon, she'd have to swim to Maui.

Still fully dressed, Jessica drifted off to sleep. She began to dream that she was walking along a deserted beach. Palm trees swayed over her head. Waves broke on the shore. In the distance she thought she saw a figure coming toward her. "Jackson!" she called. "Jackson! Here I am." She started running down the beach. And then she realized that it wasn't one figure approaching her. There were several figures. She stopped in her tracks and rubbed her eyes. Not several, but hundreds. Hundreds of girls! They were all wearing swimsuits and carrying dream books in their hands. And they weren't just walking toward her, they were running. "Jessica!" they shouted. "Jessica, wait! You have to tell us what our dreams mean!" Jessica turned and started to run in the opposite direction.

Seven

In Sweet Valley, the fastest way to spread gossip was to talk to Caroline Pearce. Unfortunately, Jean wasn't particularly friendly with Caroline. But Jessica was. So on Sunday afternoon, Jean decided to pay Jessica a visit.

"I didn't think I'd find you home on such a beautiful day," said Jean. She sat down on Jessica's bed. "I thought you always went to the beach when the weather was this good."

Jessica moaned. "I've become a slave to the world of dreams," she announced dramatically, flopping down beside Jean. "If I don't get out of here soon, I'm going to look like I've been in prison for half of my life." She examined a lock of her bright blond hair. "You don't think I'll go mousy brown because of lack of sunlight, do you?"

Jean laughed. Jessica's hair was the envy of almost every girl she knew. Except, of course, Elizabeth. "I think you're probably safe for a few more hours, Jessica," she assured her.

"I'm even dreaming about dreams," Jessica complained. "I can barely remember what Jackson looks like."

"Oops," said Jean, "maybe I shouldn't be bothering you then."

Jessica's face lit up with interest. Caroline Pearce might be the biggest gossip at Sweet Valley High, but that didn't mean that she was the only girl who was interested in the personal lives of her friends and acquaintances. "Do you mean that you've had another dream?" Jessica asked eagerly.

"Not exactly a dream," Jean said teasingly.

Now Jessica really was interested. "You don't mean—"

Jean nodded excitedly. "Uh-huh. It all came true, Jessica. Just as you said it would!"

"Wait until everybody hears about this!" Jessica squealed. "This is fantastic! You mean he actually wrote you a letter like the one in your dream?"

Jean grinned. "The one in my dream was nothing compared to the one he really sent me, Jessica." She closed her eyes and began to recite. " 'Your skin reminds me of pearls . . . your eyes are like stars . . . just to know that you might some day feel even a little for me of what I feel for you would make me the happiest person on earth.' "

Jessica pretended to swoon. "Oh my gosh, that is so romantic! But then what, Jean?" She bounced on the bed. "Have you found out who it is? Has he asked you out? Do I know him? Is he really wonderful?"

"Yes, yes, yes, yes," Jean laughed. "I know who he is. I went out with him last night. You know him, too. And he's nothing short of awesome."

"Well, who is it?" Jessica demanded. "I'm your adviser, Jean. You have to tell me!"

Jean bit her lip. "Are you really sure you want to know?"

"Jean!"

After taking a deep breath, Jean blurted out, "It's Scott Trost!"

"Scott Trost! Scott Trost wrote you a love letter?"

Jean nodded.

"Scott Trost? I don't believe it! I never really pictured him as the romantic type."

"Well, take it from me, Jessica," said Jean with a knowing smile. "If there is one thing Scott is, it's a hopeless romantic."

"Wow!"

Wow, indeed, Jean thought to herself. *With the emphasis on the word* hopeless.

Elizabeth, Enid, and Maria Santelli were sitting at a table together in the Dairi Burger, talking animatedly and drinking shakes, when they spotted Claire coming through the door.

"Hey, Claire!" Enid called as soon as she saw her. "Come on over!"

"Welcome to the singles' table." Maria grinned as Claire sat down. "Boys!" She rolled her large brown eyes. "Sometimes I think they're more trouble than they're worth."

Elizabeth winked at Claire. "Don't listen to her," she ordered. "Maria's just upset because Winston's VW broke down again and he's had to spend the weekend trying to glue it back together."

Enid made a face. "And I'm upset because this

is *another* weekend in what's beginning to seem like my perpetually single life."

"If you ask me," Elizabeth replied, "you and Claire aren't going to be alone for long." Elizabeth had seen Claire with Danny Porter twice since the three of them had met in the hall the other day. She felt pretty certain that he and Claire would get together in the very near future. And she was confident that Enid, too, would find the love she deserved.

In spite of her convictions, Elizabeth was a little surprised when Claire immediately turned to her, her eyes sparkling, and said, "Who says I don't have a boyfriend?"

Well, what do you know, thought Elizabeth. *I guess Danny's not as shy as he seems.*

"Hey, wait a minute," Maria said. "Have I missed an important Sweet Valley news flash?"

"Well, it's about time the boys in our school started showing a little sense," Enid said. She leaned across the table. "I knew they couldn't hold out against your charms for long! Now, if they'd only succumb to mine!"

Elizabeth gave Claire a hug. "I'm so happy for you," she told her. "I really am."

"Claire," Maria interrupted. "Are you going to tell us who it is, or do we have to guess?"

"Well, I'll give you a clue," Claire said. "He's devastatingly handsome."

Elizabeth smiled to herself. The others were never going to get it. Danny Porter was very good-looking, but he was so quiet and unassuming that most people really didn't notice him. What most people did notice about him was how nice he was.

Elizabeth decided to wait a little longer before astounding them with the right answer.

Maria frowned. "Bruce Patman's handsome, but he's so conceited—it can't be him."

Enid snapped her fingers. "I know, I know," she cried excitedly. "Randy Mason. It's got to be Randy Mason."

"Give up?" Claire grinned.

"All right, we give up," Enid and Maria conceded in unison.

"I don't give up," Elizabeth said. "I think—"

But her words were interrupted by Claire, who tapped a drumroll on the tabletop. "OK," she announced in a loud voice. "My new boyfriend is Scott Trost!"

"Scott Trost!" Maria exclaimed. It was clear from the expression on her face that she wouldn't have thought of Scott in a million years.

"Well, that's a surprise," Enid agreed, looking more shocked than surprised. But neither of them was half as astounded as Elizabeth.

"We went out Friday night," said Claire, "and we had a terrific time!" She looked around the table at her friends. "I mean, we just have so much in common—you know, football and Spanish class and everything. He's absolutely perfect!"

Elizabeth took a sip of her shake to stop herself from saying something she might regret. But it didn't stop her from thinking it. *Perfectly awful, you mean!*

"I guarantee you that by now the only people who haven't heard that Scott Trost has a new girlfriend are the ones who are out of town," Jean told Claire on the phone on Sunday night.

Jean was right. As soon as she had left Jessica that afternoon, Jessica phoned Caroline to tell her about Jean and Scott. Then she called Lila and Lila called Amy. Caroline took care of phoning everyone she could think of to tell them her scoop. By the time the sun had set over Sweet Valley that evening, Scott and Jean had not just gone out on one date, they were practically engaged.

And as soon as Claire had parted from her friends outside of the Dairi Burger, Maria stopped by Winston's to tell him. Enid bumped into Penny Ayala on her way home and told her. Winston told Ken Matthews. Ken told Terri. Terri ran into a few friends at the movies and told them. By the time the moon was shining over Sweet Valley that night, Scott and Claire had not just shared a double-cheese pizza, they had fallen madly in love.

By Monday morning, as Jean had predicted, Scott Trost's love life was the main topic of conversation throughout the school.

Even Elizabeth was talking about Scott. "I just can't believe it," she said to Todd as they walked to their first classes on Monday morning. "Claire Middleton and Scott Trost! What can she be thinking of? She's much too good for him."

"Oh, come on, Liz," Todd said good-naturedly. "Scott's not half as bad as you make him sound. To tell you the truth, I've always liked him. We've had a couple of good talks."

Elizabeth looked skeptical.

"He's a hard worker," Todd went on. "He's also a terrific team player." He winked. "And even *you* can't deny that he's attractive."

Elizabeth tossed her hair. "So are cobras."

"Yeah," Todd said, grinning, "but they aren't as good at football."

"They're not as arrogant, either," she retorted.

Todd put his arm around her and gave her a squeeze. "Elizabeth," he said gently, "did it ever occur to you that maybe Claire knows a side of Scott that we don't?"

Elizabeth shrugged. "All I know is that his attitude about women leaves a lot to be desired. I can't imagine what wonderful qualities you think he has that would excuse him for that."

"You're a hard woman, Elizabeth Wakefield!" Todd laughed. But then he leaned his head closer to hers and lowered his voice. "You don't happen to know who Scott's brother, Jack, is, do you?" he asked.

"Um, let's see." Elizabeth pretended to concentrate. "That wouldn't be Jack Trost, would it?" she asked innocently.

"Very funny," Todd said. "But the fact is that Scott's brother is *the* Jack Trost. You may not have heard of him, because he's a lot older than we are, but he was All-American in college. A real hero. He was all set for a brilliant professional career, but he had to give up the game because of a knee injury."

Elizabeth frowned. "I really don't see what this has to do with Scott's arrogance."

"That's what I'm trying to explain," Todd said. "I don't think it *is* arrogance. I know it sounds funny, but I think it may be just the opposite. You see, Jack Trost was a brilliant student and a gifted quarterback. He was one of those guys everything comes easily to. After he quit football,

81

he set up his own computer business, and made a success of that." Todd shook his head. "My guess is that Scott finds Jack a really hard act to follow. It's not bad enough that he thinks he has to prove something to the other Gladiators. He thinks he has to prove something to Jack, his parents, and to himself as well."

Elizabeth had listened to Todd's reasoning with interest. And she had to admit that he made a persuasive case in Scott's favor. But she was still unconvinced. "That's not a reason," she said simply. "That's only an excuse."

Cara, Lila, Jessica, and Amy were standing by Lila's locker, talking about Scott and Jean—again.

"I still can't believe it," said Amy. "One date and they're the hottest thing since chili." She made a face. "That's certainly not the Scott Trost I remember."

"I'm surprised you remember him at all, you dropped him so fast," Cara teased.

"It's all turned out like a fairy tale, hasn't it?" Jessica asked. "Love letters and secret meetings. It's just lucky I was around to interpret Jean's dreams for her, that's all I can say," she added. "Who knows what would have happened if Jean hadn't had my expert help?"

Lila moved her arm and her new gold bangle winked in the sunlight. "I, for one, have always believed in the importance of dreams," she announced.

Amy smirked. "Well, at least you got something with a good resale value out of your dream." She laughed. "I just hope, for Jean's sake, that Scott doesn't get himself kicked off the team again. It wouldn't be much of a fairy tale if the prince turned out to be a frog after all, would it?"

Cara shook her head. "That's what I really like about you, Amy. You're such an incurable romantic."

Just then someone called Jessica's name from the other end of the hall.

Jessica turned. It was Tim Nelson and Zack Johnson.

"Hey, Jessica!" Tim said when they reached her. "Zack and I have something to ask you."

"Sure," she said with a smile. "How can I help you? You have a dream you want me to analyze?"

Tim looked a little puzzled. "Well, no," he said sheepishly. "The thing is, Zack and I were wondering if you'd heard about Scott and Jean."

Jessica and her friends exchanged a look of amusement.

"Heard about them?" Jessica looked smug. "I'm the one who brought them together!"

Tim turned to Zack. "You see?" he said. "I told you you had heard wrong."

Zack shook his head. "I didn't hear wrong, Tim. Ken Matthews told me and he doesn't repeat anything he's not sure of. Anyway, he and Terri are pretty good friends with Claire. I'd think they'd know if she was going out with someone or not."

"Claire?" said Jessica. "What does Claire have to do with this?"

John Pfeifer, the sports editor of *The Oracle*, stopped Elizabeth on her way into English class.

"I don't want to make you late or anything," he said, "but I was wondering if you could clear something up for me."

"What is it, John?" asked Elizabeth. "Something to do with the paper?"

"Uh-uh." He shook his head. "I was just wondering if you'd heard that Scott Trost and Claire Middleton are a couple."

Elizabeth nodded. "Yes," she said, "that's what I heard."

John scratched his head. "Do you mind if I ask you who told you?"

"Well of course not," Elizabeth shifted her books in her arms. "Claire told me."

"Claire?" John repeated as though he hadn't heard her right. "Claire told you herself?"

"That's right, John. Why?"

A lopsided grin appeared on John's face. "Well, because Dana says she heard that *Jean* and Scott are an item."

"But that's impossible!" Elizabeth exclaimed.

"Impossible or not," John said, his grin spreading, "Dana says she was told by a reliable source."

"And who would that be?"

John winked. "Jessica Wakefield."

Jean entered the cafeteria that afternoon just as she usually did. She came in from the west side, her books in her arms, and stopped in the doorway to see where her friends were sitting. Only that day her friends weren't sitting anywhere. Jessica, Amy, Lila, and Cara were striding across the room toward her, talking excitedly among themselves. Jean hid a smile. Jessica's eyes were flashing and her mouth was set in a determined line. *Well*, Jean said to herself, *it looks like the news has gotten around about Scott and Claire!*

Jean smiled as they approached. "Hi," she said. "Are we eating outside today?"

They came to an abrupt stop in front of her.

"Jean!" Jessica demanded. "Jean, have you heard that Claire Middleton's been going around telling everyone that she's dating Scott Trost?"

"Uh, I . . ." Jean stammered.

"It's true," Amy said. "Claire's trying to steal your boyfriend."

"It's too bad Jessica didn't see this in one of your dreams," added Lila. "But I guess we all have our limitations."

"Never mind that," Jessica said firmly. "You've got to have a talk with Claire right away, Jean. You've got to set her straight!"

"And here's your opportunity." Amy pointed to the other side of the cafeteria, where Claire had just walked in through the door.

Jessica slipped her arm through Jean's. "Come on," she said. "We'll be right beside you for moral support."

Claire had only taken three steps into the cafeteria when she, too, found herself surrounded by well-meaning friends.

Elizabeth said, "I've got to talk to you, Claire."

Claire smiled. "Well, sure, Elizabeth. Do you think I could get my lunch first?"

"I wish I'd said something to you yesterday,"

Elizabeth said, half to Claire and half to herself. "I should have known something like this would happen."

"Elizabeth," Claire said gently, "if I could just get something to eat . . ."

But Elizabeth shook her head. "This is too important," she said. "We have to discuss it *right now*." She lowered her voice. "I don't know if you've heard the rumors, but Jean's been telling everyone that *she's* going out with Scott."

Claire blushed. "Well, actually, I did hear something."

"*Something?*" Enid asked. "*Something?* It's all over the school!"

"Claire," Elizabeth insisted, "you have got to talk to Scott before this thing goes any further."

"I—" Claire started to say.

"I think you should talk to Jean as well," Enid said. "After all, she's as much a victim in this thing as you are. He's taking advantage of both of you."

"Well, sure—"

"First things first, though," Elizabeth said firmly. "And if my eyes don't deceive me, there's the first thing now."

Winston leaned over to Maria, pointing discreetly at Scott Trost, casually strolling into the cafeteria. "Uh-oh," he whispered. "Gunfight at the Sweet Valley Corral."

But of all the students in the cafeteria, Scott seemed to be the one least concerned by what was going on. If anything, he seemed pleased, not worried. Apparently aware that almost every eye in the room had turned to him the moment

86

he stepped through the door, he pulled himself up to his full height, stuck out his chin, and broadened his smile.

Jean couldn't believe how well things were going. Everything was happening exactly as she and Claire had planned! Now all she had to do was march over there and wipe that smug smile from Scott Trost's face. Jean took a deep breath and, followed by her friends, marched across the room.

"Just what kind of game are you playing, Scott Trost?" Jean demanded in a loud, clear voice. "I thought you told me that *I* was your girlfriend!"

"Just a minute!" Claire shouted, coming up from the other side. "What about me? You told me *I* was the one you liked!"

Scott looked from one girl to the other, and then back again.

Total silence had fallen around them. *This is perfect!* Jean thought. She had gone over this moment so many times, she knew exactly what would happen next. Scott would become embarrassed and then he would apologize. People would start to laugh at him. In the end, he would run from the cafeteria and she and Claire would embrace each other victoriously.

And then Scott's voice interrupted her thoughts.

"Hey, ladies," he said, smooth as ice. "Don't yell at me."

Jean blinked. What was wrong with this picture? Scott wasn't embarrassed. He wasn't apologizing. He wasn't making any excuses. Why, he almost seemed to be enjoying himself!

"If you ask me," he continued, "anything worth having is worth fighting for, right?"

If this was begging for forgiveness, Jean thought, he was certainly going about it in an unusual way.

Jessica leaned closer to Jean. "Did he say what I thought he just said?" she whispered.

Elizabeth gave Claire a tiny shove. "Don't let him talk to you like that!" she hissed.

But before either girl could make a move, Scott started to talk again. "I've got an idea," he said coolly. "How about a little competition?"

Claire looked at Jean.

"A little competition?" Jean repeated dully.

Scott nodded. "Yeah. If each of you wants to be my girlfriend so badly, then why don't you each try to win me? I'll go out with one of you one night and the other one the next night. Then I'll decide who I like best and I'll take her to the dance."

"Do the girls a favor, why don't you?" Winston Egbert said in a loud whisper.

"Claire," Elizabeth hissed. "What's wrong with you?"

But Claire seemed to be waiting for Jean to take the lead.

Jean's mind was racing. First she told herself that she should have her head examined for ever having had one kind thought about this creep. Then she got an idea. There might still be a way for them to really even the score with this conceited chauvinist.

She forced her lips into a smile. "You're on!" she said to Scott. While her friends were still staring at her, open-mouthed, she turned to Claire. "You'd better start worrying, Claire Middleton," Jean declared. "This is one competition you're not going to win!"

Eight

Todd had had to stay after class and talk to his math teacher, so that by the time he entered the cafeteria on that Monday afternoon, the confrontation was over and the smoke had cleared. He saw Elizabeth sitting with Enid and he waved. Enid waved back. Elizabeth didn't see him. She seemed to be engrossed in something she was saying. Todd got his lunch and crossed the cafeteria to their table. "Hi," he said as he put down his tray. He leaned down to give Elizabeth a kiss on the cheek, expecting her to turn to him with a happy smile.

Elizabeth turned to him, but there was no happy smile on her lips. Her cheeks were pink. "Did you hear any of that?" she wanted to know. Todd noticed that her eyes were the color of a stormy sea.

"Excuse me?" he asked politely. "Did I hear any of what?"

Enid grimaced. "Did you miss a scene!" she said. "It was like something in a movie."

Todd looked at Elizabeth. "I take it this movie wasn't a comedy," he joked.

"It was a farce," Elizabeth said. "That's what it was. A farce." She sighed deeply. "Oh, Todd, it was just awful!" Elizabeth explained the scene with Scott, Claire, and Jean in full detail.

"Can you believe it?" she fumed when she was done. "He just stood there with this arrogant smile on his face!" She shook her head as though she still couldn't completely believe it herself. "A competition to go out with Scott Trost!" she exploded. "Maybe now you'll agree with me that boys are more selfish and shallow than girls."

But Todd shook his head. "No, I don't. Look, from what you've told me, I'd have to agree that Scott behaved like a complete creep. But what about Claire and Jean?" he asked. "They went along with it, didn't they?"

"Only because he put them on the spot," Elizabeth said. But even as she was defending the girls' behavior to Todd, she couldn't figure Jean and Claire out. Why would two sensible, attractive girls fight over such a conceited jerk? It didn't make sense at all.

Lila sat down in the shade of an oak tree and looked around. "Where's Jean?" she asked. After the scene in the cafeteria, the girls had decided to eat outdoors.

Jessica sat down beside Cara. "She said she forgot something in her locker. She'll be right back."

Cara shook her head. "Poor thing," she sympathized. "Did you ever see anything like that in your entire life? Scott actually *wants* them to fight over him!" She wrenched her sandwich from its wrapper. "No wonder Jean's upset."

"She didn't seem upset to me," Jessica commented. "She looked a little surprised at first, but by the end, I thought she seemed to be pretty much in control."

"Anyway," Lila said authoritatively, "Jean has nothing to be upset about. She did the right thing." She brushed aside a fly. "To tell the truth, I really don't see what the fuss is all about. There's nothing wrong with a little competition. That's what life's all about, isn't it? Competition."

Amy nodded. "Competition is what being popular is all about," she said. "I mean, let's be realistic. We had to compete to become cheerleaders. We had to compete to join Pi Beta Alpha."

A smile of understanding lit up Jessica's face. "If you think about it, when someone asks you out, it means you've won a competition with all the *other* girls he could have asked out. We're competing all the time!"

Cara stared dubiously at the hard-boiled egg she held in her hand. "I'm not so sure that's the same thing as setting up a contest to decide who to take to a dance," she said.

"Don't be silly, Cara. Of course it is," Lila argued.

"If you think about it, it's a little more honest, really," Jessica pointed out.

"Absolutely," Lila said approvingly.

"And it's not as though Jean won't win," Amy added. "She's prettier, isn't she? You don't seriously think Scott's going to choose a quarterback over a cheerleader, do you?"

The image of Scott and Claire, both of them wearing Gladiators uniforms, sitting side by side in the movie theater, seemed to float in the blue sky above them. Lila, Cara, and Jessica began to laugh.

"Oh, don't," Lila gasped, "it's *too* funny. Can't you just see their helmets crashing together when they try to kiss?"

"We've got to tell Jean that we're behind her one hundred percent," Jessica said when she finally caught her breath. "There's no way Claire can win over one of us."

Cara looked toward the building. "I wonder what's taking Jean so long."

"She's probably in the girls' room, checking her makeup or brushing her hair," Jessica said. She picked a leaf out of her lunch. "Where else would she be?"

Jean *was* in the girls' room, and so was Claire. But neither of them was crying her eyes out or touching up her lipstick. Instead, they were clutching each other and laughing uproariously.

"There was a minute there when you even had *me* fooled." Claire grinned.

"I was hoping you'd figure out what I was up to," Jean said. "I'm just so glad you followed my lead!"

"Don't think it was easy," Claire said. "Not with Elizabeth right behind me, telling me to stand up to him. I just hope I can get through my date with him tonight without giving the game away."

"You'll be fine," Jean said. "But I think we'd

better establish a couple of ground rules before we go any further. Scott may have come up with the idea for this competition, but we can play the game however we want."

"Absolutely." Claire nodded in agreement. "I was thinking that myself. For instance, I don't think we should let him kiss either of us. We'll tell him it's not OK until he's made his decision."

"And we'll both be as nice as we can to him, so he doesn't suspect it's all a trick," Jean said. "But there'll be no kissing and no holding hands."

"And he has to announce his decision publicly," added Claire. "The day before the dance."

"There's no question about that," Jean said determinedly. "I want the entire school to be there when we both turn him down."

The end-of-period bell rang. "Uh-oh," Claire said. "I didn't realize it was so late!"

"Me, neither." Jean laughed. "I guess time really does fly when you're having fun!"

"Oh, don't say that." Claire groaned. "That means my date with Toad Trost is going to feel about three weeks long."

Jean went through the motions of the rest of the day, but it was as though her mind and her body belonged to separate people. Her body had finished school and gotten a lift home with Sandy. Her body had helped her mother do a little gardening and had eaten supper. But her mind hadn't been involved in any of it.

Her mind had been on Scott. She couldn't think of anything else. All afternoon, her anger toward him had grown and grown.

Jean had no idea at all what she had for dinner, but when it was over, she excused herself to go to her room and do her homework. She spread her books out on her bed, turned her notebook to a clean page, and opened her math textbook to that day's assignment. Jean leaned back on the bed. She was supposed to be thinking of x and y, and instead all she could think of was S and T!

She closed her eyes.

She was sitting in the Corvette next to Scott. They were on their way to pick up Claire.

"You know what I don't understand, Scott?" Jean said. "I don't understand how you're going to score us."

Scott winked. "No problem. I've got everything under control." He held up a small red notebook. "Look," he said. "I've got a system all worked out!"

Jean took the book in her hands. He had divided the page into two columns. One was headed *Jean*. The other was headed *Claire*. Down the side of each page was a list of categories: promptness, dress, hair, personality, mood, interest, conversation, humor. . . . The list seemed to go on forever.

They pulled up in front of Claire's house and walked up the path. Mrs. Middleton opened the door. "Oh, I'm sorry, Scott," Mrs. Middleton said. "Claire's not ready yet." Scott took out his notebook and gave Claire a minus five for promptness.

When Claire finally did come downstairs, apologizing profusely, she looked extremely pretty in a blue skirt and matching top. Scott took out his notebook again and gave her an eight. "I can't go giving tens away," he joked to Jean. "I'm the only one who's perfect."

Jean sat in the back seat as they drove to the movie. It seemed a little strange to her, going on their date with them, but Claire didn't seem to notice that she was there. She listened as Claire and Scott talked. Claire was disagreeing with Scott about their favorite bands. Scott shook his head. "I don't think you understand, Claire," Scott told her solemnly. "I'm going to have to deduct points if you can't do better than that."

"Oh, no, Scott," Claire pleaded. "Don't do that. I'm sorry I disagreed with you, I really am."

After they'd bought their tickets for the movie, they went to buy a snack. But they couldn't agree whether to get the popcorn Scott wanted or the chocolate bar Claire wanted.

"Why can't you have popcorn and I'll have the candy?" Claire suggested.

Scott shook his head. He opened his notebook on the counter. "I'm afraid that's not good enough, Claire," he said. "You can't expect me to give a high score to a girl who doesn't like popcorn, can you?"

"But that's not fair!" Jean shouted. "That's not fair! That's not fair!"

The telephone began to ring. "Answer the phone, Jean," Scott ordered. "Answer the phone or you'll lose points for laziness!"

Jean woke with a start and picked up the receiver.

"Hi," Claire said brightly. "I just got home."

Jean pulled herself together. She rubbed her eyes and peered at her watch. It said ten-forty-five. "How was it?" she asked. "Did everything go OK?"

"We didn't have pizza," Claire said, "but other than that, it was pretty much like our first date." She sighed. "It was all right, I guess. If you don't mind dates that seem to last a month and a half."

Jean smiled. Maybe they should start scoring *Scott*, she thought. Minus fifty for originality!

Nine

"So where are you two going tonight?" Sandy asked.

Jessica, Amy, Lila, and Cara looked at Jean with interest. Jean tried to look a little more excited than she felt. "I'm not sure," she replied truthfully. "We haven't decided."

Jessica waved her apple in Jean's direction. "You really should find out before school is over, you know," she told her friend. "You want to wear the right clothes."

"She's got a point," Sandy agreed. "You've got to look absolutely perfect."

"I don't think Jean has to worry about that," Jessica said. "She *always* looks perfect."

"It's unnatural." Cara laughed. "An hour after I leave the house my clothes start looking lived-in. But you always manage to look immaculate." She shook her head ruefully. "Why don't your clothes wrinkle like everybody else's? Why don't you ever spill anything on yourself?"

"Don't look *too* good," Amy advised. "You don't want him to like you too much or he'll want to kiss you."

"And what's wrong with that?" Cara demanded. "Jean's going to have to kiss him sometime. How else is she going to know if he likes her and if she really likes him?"

"All I'm saying is that Jean doesn't have to be in any *hurry* to kiss Scott." Amy frowned. "Take it from me, he is *not* a great kisser."

"And who would know better," Cara joked, "but the girl who's done the survey?"

Amy pretended that Cara hadn't spoken. "Well, I'd wait for at least one more date," she advised. "You might as well get him to take you to a couple of nice places before you learn the terrible truth."

Sandy shook her head. "Oh, no. I think Jean should wait until Scott's made his decision. She doesn't want him kissing her one night and kissing Claire the next."

"That's a good point," Cara agreed.

"Absolutely." Jessica sighed. "Once Jackson and I start dating, I know it would drive me nuts if I thought he was kissing someone else."

Jean and Sandy exchanged a puzzled look. Was this the same Jessica Wakefield who had always said that she didn't want a steady boyfriend because variety was the spice of life?

Lila brushed a few crumbs from her blouse. "Would you like a little free advice, Jean?" she asked, taking charge of the conversation.

A reluctant smile spread across Jean's face. The last thing she needed was advice from Lila

Fowler, but she was too polite to say so. Instead she said, "Sure."

Lila leaned back in her chair. "Well, I think there are two rules you should follow if you want to beat Claire."

"This should be good," Cara whispered to Sandy.

Lila began counting off the two rules on her fingers. "One, always let him choose where you're going."

"Wait a minute, Lila," Jessica protested. "What if he wants to do something Jean doesn't want to do?"

"Yeah." Sandy smiled. "Say he wants to do a hundred sit-ups?"

Lila shook her head firmly. "If it's something you can't do, then you *watch* him do it."

"You mean just like you would? Lila, you wouldn't ride in a ten-year-old car, let alone do anything that might break your nails!"

"That's different," Lila said evenly.

"You mean because it's you," Cara teased.

Lila pursed her lips. "No, because this is a competition. The idea is to beat Claire, not to have a good time."

Cara gave Jean a wink. "And don't you forget that, either!"

Jean smiled, but on the inside she sighed. She comforted herself with the thought that things couldn't get any worse than they already were. Not only was she in a contest with a girl she liked for a boy she disliked, but she was being given advice by Lila. There was nowhere to go from here but up. "What's the second rule?" Jean asked.

"That's simple," Lila said happily. "Rule two: If you do something, like play miniature golf, you should always let him win."

There was a chorus of groans from her friends.

"Oh, come on, Lila," Amy argued. "That is so old-fashioned. You can't really be serious."

"Of course I'm serious," Lila protested. "If Jean wants to impress him, she has to let him take charge. And she has to make sure that *he* looks good. She can't show him up by being better at things than he is. A boy doesn't *want* to have to compete with his date."

"Don't listen to Lila, Jean," Jessica said. "I know all about getting boys interested—"

"Well, I'm glad to hear you know all about something," Amy interrupted.

"And just what's that supposed to mean?" Jessica asked sharply.

"You know what it means," Amy replied sweetly. "You aren't exactly the expert on dreams that you claim to be, are you, Jessica?"

Jessica's eyes flashed, but otherwise she remained cool. "All right, so a couple of my interpretations have been a little off."

Amy laughed. "A *little*?" she shrieked. "Oh, Jessica, really. You were wrong about Robin taking a trip. You were wrong about Andrea Slade getting a new car."

Cara and Lila started laughing, too.

"And what about when you told me I was going to be on television?" Cara asked between giggles.

"And didn't I hear something about a weekend in Acapulco?" Lila added.

Jessica held up her hands for silence. "All right,

all right," she said loudly. "I thought we were supposed to be helping Jean prepare for her date, not criticizing me."

But Jean's head was spinning from all the conflicting advice. "That's all right." Jean laughed. "I think you've helped me enough!"

"I can't remember the last time we had a response like this," Penny Ayala said to Elizabeth.

The two girls were standing at the desk Penny used as editor of *The Oracle.* On top of it was a pile of letters from students who had read Elizabeth's recent article about what boys and girls were looking for when they dated.

Elizabeth shook her head. "You mean these all came this morning?"

Penny smiled. "That's right. I thought the ones I gave you yesterday were going to be it, but as you can see, I was very wrong. And what's really surprising is that most of them are from boys. This one's so good, in fact, that I was thinking I might run it in the next issue."

Elizabeth peered over Penny's shoulder. The letter was neatly typed and headed: "Is It True That Boys See Better Than They Think?"

"Listen to this." Penny began to read. " 'Many girls think that boys seem to prefer beauty to brains, but is this really true? Of course, if you ask a guy what it is that first gets him interested in a girl, he'll say it's her looks. But if we're honest with ourselves, we'll admit that we're *all* interested in how people look. How could we not be? Unless you're blind, it's the first thing you notice about someone else. If you are blind, I guess the first thing you probably notice is what kind of toothpaste or deodorant the other person uses. But if you have sight, you use it. The point is that beauty is in the eye of the beholder. Not only that, but everybody knows that what we see is never the whole picture. There's a lot more to everyone than what he or she looks like. It's only *after* you're attracted to someone because of how they look that you can find out if you're really interested in them or not because of the *type* of person they are.' "

Penny put the letter down and smiled. She put a hand on Elizabeth's shoulder. "My star reporter does it again!" She laughed. "I really have to congratulate you on coming up with such a thought-provoking piece."

The letter made Elizabeth feel slightly embarrassed—not because it wasn't convincing, but because it was too convincing. It said all the things that Todd had been trying to tell her, but that she had tried to ignore.

"To tell you the truth," Elizabeth said, "between this letter and the ones I took home to read last night, I've had my own thoughts provoked as well." She smiled wryly. "Maybe the results of my questionnaire weren't as conclusive as I thought." She was beginning to realize that there were quite a few girls who were only interested in boys because they were cute or superjocks, and quite a few boys who weren't really interested in looks at all. Maybe she had been a little too quick to put all the blame on boys.

"Well, if you want to write a follow-up piece, you're more than welcome," Penny said. "In fact, it would be great. It would give us a chance to use the picture Claire took of you and Todd, which we didn't have room for last time. Maybe we could run it with extracts from your answers to the questionnaire."

"Um . . ." Elizabeth said slowly, "I'll have to ask Todd what he thinks about that idea." She hadn't spoken to him since the previous day in the cafeteria, when she had been so upset about Scott Trost.

"Sure," Penny said, "ask him." Then she noticed the worried look on Elizabeth's face. "Hey, you two haven't had a fight, have you?"

Elizabeth shook her head. "No, we haven't had a fight." She made a face. "But we haven't exactly *not* had a fight, either."

Scott arrived at Jean's house at seven-thirty. From her bedroom window, Jean watched him walk from the car to the house. He was wearing jeans and a sports shirt, and, as far as she could tell, he wasn't carrying a notebook. *What's confusing*, Jean thought, *is that he looks so human.*

What was even more confusing, however, was that he was acting so human. By the time she came downstairs, he was sitting in the living room with her mother, discussing shrubs. He got to his feet when she entered the room, complimented her on the way she looked, and opened the car door for her. Then he waved to her mother, who was standing on the porch watching them drive away, no doubt thinking what a nice boy he was.

"Well," he said, glancing over at her almost shyly, "what would you like to do, Jean?"

Jean had given a lot of thought to what her

friends had said at lunch. It was true: if anyone knew how to impress a boy, it was they. Particularly Lila and Jessica. Therefore, because she didn't want to impress Scott, she would pay no attention to what they had said. Because she didn't care what Scott thought of her, she would go out of her way to make him miserable. If there had been some way of discovering the color he hated most and the scent that gave him a rash, she would have been wearing them. And because she would rather have been doing her math homework than going out with him, she was going to make sure they did things she enjoyed, particularly if they were things she knew he didn't enjoy. "I was thinking it might be fun to play miniature golf."

"Miniature golf?" he repeated.

Jean smiled. She had been talking to Ken Matthews that afternoon and he had made a joke about not blowing the contest by making Scott play miniature golf. "Yes," she said chirpily. "Miniature golf. That's what I'd like to do."

But to her surprise, Scott didn't argue or suggest an alternative. "OK." He grinned. "If that's what you want to do, that's what we'll do. But I'm warning you right now that the last time I played, I spent twenty minutes at the windmill, and I never did get through."

This time he spent twenty-five minutes at the windmill, until finally, in desperation, Jean grabbed the club from his hands and hit his ball through.

She thought he would refuse to play anymore after that. She had been a cheerleader long enough to know that superjocks didn't like to take help from anyone, especially a girl.

But she was wrong. "I told you I wasn't any good at this." Scott laughed. "I'm hopeless at anything that's not football."

In spite of herself, Jean felt herself warming up to him again. "Unfortunately, I'm not dressed for football," she joked back. "I left my helmet home."

"Then I guess you're going to have to give me a little coaching so I don't spend the rest of the night on hole eleven!"

After Jean had beaten him, they decided to stop for pizza. He wanted pepperoni and she wanted anchovy. At Scott's suggestion, they compromised and got mushroom.

"You're a terrific coach," he told her as their pizza arrived.

She smiled back. "I can't be that terrific. You lost the game."

"Yeah," he shrugged, "but I had a lot of fun doing it."

Jean tried to hide her surprise. "You had fun?"

He nodded. "Yeah, I had a great time. Did you see that guy's face when my ball jumped over the wall and into the hole he was playing?"

The memory made her laugh. "I thought it was pretty funny when you nearly hit me with your club."

"I was trying to impress you with my back-swing." Scott grinned.

Somehow Scott's hand had found its way on top of hers. It felt so natural that she didn't even notice it at first.

She pulled her hand away and looked at her watch. "We'd better hurry up," she said briskly. "After all, you've got a breakfast date with Claire, don't you? I wouldn't want you to be too tired for that."

"Jean," Scott said softly, the smile gone from his face, "about this thing with Claire—I'd like to try to explain."

"I've got to go to the ladies' room," Jean said quickly. "Excuse me."

"OK," Scott said glumly. "I'll get the check."

Mission accomplished, she congratulated herself as she hurried from the table. *At last he looks as miserable as he deserves to be!*

Elizabeth came into her sister's room to say goodnight. Jessica was sprawled on the bed, flipping through a magazine.

"What's this?" Elizabeth teased. "Shouldn't you be analyzing dreams or packing for your trip to Maui?"

"I wish." Jessica pushed herself up on her elbows. "Really, Elizabeth, can you believe it? Just because a couple of my interpretations were wrong, everyone's acting as if it's all my fault."

"Well, Jessica," Elizabeth said gently, "you did tell everyone that you were an expert."

Jessica waved this detail aside. "And to top it all off," she continued, "not only have I not made a dime, I've lost money paying for those flyers!" She pulled the pillow over her head.

Elizabeth lifted a corner of the pillow. "It isn't really that bad," she said soothingly.

Jessica moaned. "It isn't that bad? It isn't that

bad? Elizabeth, I don't think you understand what this means."

"It means that you've wasted a few days, Jessica, that's all."

Jessica moaned again. "No, it doesn't. It means I'm going to wind up an old maid, because I'm never going to get to Hawaii to find the man of my dreams."

Ten

On Wednesday morning Jean was waiting by the bike racks for Claire to arrive at school, fresh from her breakfast date with Scott. Jean tapped her foot. She checked her watch. What were they having for breakfast, a three-course meal? If they didn't hurry they'd be late for their first class. She tried to imagine Scott and Claire. Where were they right at this minute? She checked her watch again. What were they talking about? Jean tapped her foot again. What were they saying about her? Was Scott behaving so arrogantly that Claire was ready to slam the car door on his hand? Or was he being so charming that Claire was forgetting it was all a game?

Jean was just about to give up and head to her class when she caught sight of Claire rushing toward her.

"Where have you been?" Jean asked. "I was starting to worry that something had happened."

"You thought something might have happened

on a date with Scott?" Claire asked sarcastically. "You must be kidding."

Jean walked along beside Claire. "So how was it? Any better than the last one?"

"Only for the fact that I had to take a bus to school, it was exactly the same. Oh, yeah. And we had doughnuts instead of pizza."

"You had to take a bus here?" Jean asked. "What happened to the Corvette?"

Claire pushed a strand of hair from her face. "The Corvette's at the animal clinic with Scott."

Jean came to a stop. "The animal clinic? What are you talking about, Claire?"

Reluctantly, Claire stopped walking, too. "On the way back from breakfast, we found an injured dog on the side of the road," she explained. "And Scott insisted on taking it to a vet."

"Well," Jean said slowly, "that was a nice thing to do." Why was he always doing things to show her he wasn't a monster, she wondered?

"I know it was a nice thing to do, Jean, but we've got a Spanish quiz first period." She shrugged. "And it wasn't as if the dog were dying or anything. He'd hurt his paw. We could have called the number on the dog's tag and had his owners come and get him." She made a face. "But no, Macho Man has a thing about dogs and he wouldn't leave it there by itself." She started to walk again. "Look, I've got to hurry, Jean. I'll talk to you tonight after your date, OK?"

"Sure," Jean said. "I'll call you tonight." As she watched Claire hurry off to class, Jean thought about Scott. Even though he had a quiz that morning, and even though he needed to keep his average up to stay on the football team, he had chosen to take an injured dog to the vet. Jean took a deep breath and started toward class. There was no getting away from it: she was beginning to feel like the heel she had accused Scott of being.

Jessica left her English class feeling as though a truck had just rolled over her. No, she corrected herself, not a truck, a surfboard. A large pink surfboard. She groaned. How could she have forgotten all about her English project? She had begun it more than a week earlier, but she'd gotten so involved with her dream business that it had completely slipped from her mind. And the project wasn't something she could cobble together in one or two evenings. She was supposed to have made up a mock travel brochure to illustrate the skills she had learned in the class's work on media and communications. Jessica knew it would take *days* to gather the information and actually put it all together, and she also knew her parents would not be happy about this. They were always lecturing her about being more responsible and taking more interest in her schoolwork. How had she gotten herself in such a mess? Now she was *really* going to have to work if she hoped to hand in her project on time.

Then, just as Jessica was preparing herself for another groan, she caught a glimpse of something dark and dreamy at the other end of the hall. It was Steve Anderson. Her English project was not the only thing she had been neglecting, she realized suddenly. She had been so full of her plans for going to Hawaii and meeting Jackson that she had left herself without a date for the big Love in

Bloom dance on Saturday. She tossed her head and put a bright smile on her lips. Steve smiled back. *OK, Jessica!* she thought. *Maybe it isn't too late to accept Steve's invitation to the dance.* She started walking faster. He started moving toward her.

"Hi!" he called excitedly. "I was hoping to run into you."

"Hi!" she called back. "I—" Her words faded into the noise of the hallway. Steve Anderson had walked right past her to talk to some other girl behind her! *Love in Bloom!* Jessica muttered to herself. *It's more like Ragweed in Bloom!* She stomped toward her next class. Dreams, she decided, definitely weren't all they were cracked up to be!

"Well, what do you think?" Elizabeth said to Todd. "Do you mind if Penny runs our picture in the next issue with some of the answers to the questionnaire?"

Todd shook his head. "Of course I don't mind. But what I'd really like to see is this letter you were telling me about. The one about whether or not boys see better than they think."

"You'll see it in *The Oracle*," she said shortly. Elizabeth had told Todd about the letter because she'd been feeling bad about being so hard on him when he had tried to defend Scott. But the truth was that though she had mentioned the letter to him in a general way, she still really didn't want to talk about it in any depth. She couldn't quite bring herself to admit to Todd that she had been, in some part, wrong.

"And are you going to answer it in *The Oracle*?" Todd persisted.

"Answer it?" Elizabeth repeated. "Well, I don't know. I really hadn't thought about actually answering it."

"I think it would be a good idea." Todd smiled. "It would be very interesting to hear your reply." He gave her a little nudge. "You do think the guy who wrote this letter is wrong, don't you?"

Elizabeth avoided his eyes. "Oh, well," she mumbled, "I wouldn't say that he's *completely* wrong. I told you, Todd, he made some very good points."

"Then I think you owe it to your readers to reply."

Elizabeth gave Todd a kiss on the cheek. "And I think I owe it to myself not to be late for class," she said, and hurried away.

Despite her change of heart, the minute Elizabeth saw Claire walking down the hall on her way to lunch, she felt her anger rise up again. They hadn't really spoken since the showdown on Monday, and Elizabeth was hoping that maybe by now Claire had changed her mind about going out with Scott.

"Claire!" she called. "Claire! Wait up!"

Claire turned with a smile. "Hi, Elizabeth. What's happening?"

"Oh, nothing much," Elizabeth said noncommittally. "How about you?"

"You don't fool me, Elizabeth Wakefield," Claire said with a smile. "You mean, am I still going through with this competition, don't you?"

"I know it's not really any of my business, Claire," Elizabeth said hurriedly, "but it really

112

upsets me to see two people as nice as you and Jean throw yourselves at an arrogant creep like Scott Trost."

Claire laughed. "Can you keep a secret, Elizabeth?" she asked in a whisper.

Elizabeth nodded. "Of course I can," she promised.

Claire looked around to make sure that no one else was listening. "Well, the truth is, Elizabeth, Jean and I knew all about Scott's game practically right from the start." As they walked along, Claire told Elizabeth all about the identical letters and the plan she and Jean had come up with to teach Scott a lesson.

"Whew," Elizabeth sighed. "What a relief! You really had me worried. I don't know which makes me happier, the thought that you and Jean aren't really being used, or the thought that Scott is."

"I just wish it were all over," Claire said wearily. "I think the strain of it is beginning to get to me. It's gone on a lot longer than I thought it would."

"I can imagine," Elizabeth sympathized. "Having to be nice to Scott day after day can't be much fun."

Claire grinned. "Oh, it's not that," she explained. "He's not nearly as bad as he makes you think. It's just that . . . well . . . you know." Claire came to a halt. Her cheeks were bright pink. "It's just that in case somebody else is thinking of asking me to the dance, it would be nice if he didn't think I was serious about Scott."

Elizabeth was just about to mention Danny Porter when she saw Danny himself strolling down the empty hallway toward them. *Maybe I should get in on these love games, too,* Elizabeth thought. She waited until Danny was close enough to hear and then she said, "Well, I'm really glad to hear that you're not interested in Scott after all."

Danny stopped in his tracks.

"You're not, are you, Claire?" Elizabeth prompted.

Claire stared at her in surprise. "Well, no, I just told you—"

"Oh, my gosh," Elizabeth said suddenly. "Look at the time. I promised Todd I'd meet him for lunch. I'd better run."

She hurried on and then looked back over her shoulder. Claire and Danny were deep in conversation. *I guess Jessica isn't the only romantic twin in the Wakefield family after all!* she thought happily. *Or the only one capable of meddling in other people's lives, either.*

"I thought we'd go somewhere a little more romantic than a miniature-golf course," Scott said as Jean got into the car that night. He shut the door and leaned against the window frame. "That is, unless you've got something else in mind?" he asked softly. He reached out to touch her hair. Jean pulled back from his hand so quickly that she whacked her head against the headrest.

All day long Jean had been flipping back and forth between remembering how angry she was with Scott and feeling bad because she was leading him on. And it was all his fault, she thought. Why couldn't he pick a way to behave and then stick to it, instead of laughing at himself and rescuing injured dogs? "Oh, no," she said quickly, "a romantic evening sounds just great."

On the way to the restaurant, Jean asked Scott how his day had been. She thought that if he talked about himself he might mention Claire, and if he mentioned Claire, she would be able to remind herself how much she disliked him. But Scott talked about the dog. How sad it had looked sitting by the roadside. How much pain it had been in. How he had held it while the vet set its paw.

Has he found out about our plan? she wondered. *Is he doing this on purpose to throw me off?*

"But that must have taken ages!" Jean said. "Didn't you say you had a Spanish quiz this morning!"

Scott made a face. "Adios, amigo." He laughed. "Luckily, I explained everything to Mrs. Ray and she's going to let me make it up tomorrow afternoon." He pretended to wipe sweat from his brow. "I can't tell you what a relief that is. My parents wouldn't have been as understanding as Mrs. Ray. They don't think anything is more important than getting ahead."

Jean watched his profile as he drove. "But you disagree?"

Scott didn't answer. He pulled into the restaurant's parking lot and turned off the engine. "Voilà!" he cried. "The most romantic French restaurant in Southern California!"

But once they were inside the Côte d'Or in Malvina, Jean found she was in a worse state than ever. Should she call off the contest and tell him the truth? If she told him the truth, would he ever

115

speak to her again? Did she care if he ever spoke to her again?

Scott pushed her chair in toward the table. "What do you think?" he asked. The room was dimly lit and beautifully decorated in shades of blue and white. "I figured that with your sense of style, you'd probably like it here," Scott explained.

Jean was so overwhelmed by Scott's courteous behavior, she accidentally knocked over her water glass.

Scott, just about to sit down, quickly started mopping up the spilled water.

"Oh, no," Jean protested. "I'm so sorry. Let me do that." But as she reached for her napkin, her hand collided with the candle, sending it crashing across the table.

Scott pulled his hand out of the way just in time. "Hey," he teased, "what are you trying to do, kill me?" He leaned over and picked the candle up from the floor, placing it carefully on the table.

She knew that the look on her face was saying, *I'm not sure that's such a bad idea.*

Suddenly, the smile left Scott's face. "Not that I'd blame you if you did want to kill me," he said slowly. "Not after the way I've treated you and Claire."

Jean picked up her menu and hid behind it.

"Jean," he said gently. "Jean, we've got to talk about this. I tried last night, but you didn't want to listen then, either."

Jean's lower lip was trembling. She kept her face hidden behind the menu. "There's nothing to talk about. Claire and I agreed to the contest and that's that."

"No, it isn't," he argued. He tugged the menu away from her face.

"Yes, it is." Jean drew the menu back up.

"Jean, you've got to listen to me. I know I've behaved like a real creep, writing those letters to the two of you and setting up this stupid competition." Once again, Scott pulled the menu away from her face. "But you've got to believe me when I say I wish I'd sent only one letter, and that I'd sent it to you."

For a moment all Jean could see was the candlelight sparkling around them and the look of warmth and sincerity in Scott's deep blue eyes. She felt as though she were floating. If violins had started to play behind her at that moment, she wouldn't have been surprised. But then she remembered whose deep blue eyes she was staring into: the eyes of Toad Trost, the two-timer. She smiled sweetly. "But you didn't write only one letter," she reminded him gently.

"Jean," he implored her, "I'm trying to apologize."

"You wrote two." Jean turned her attention back to the appetizers. "What do you recommend?" she asked him. "The fried cheese or the shrimp?"

Jessica dug through six piles of clothes and possessions before she found the beginnings of her English project. If it could be called a beginning. What it was, in fact, was a magazine with a feature article on Mexico. She had thought at the time that she would make a brochure on Mexico. After all, she had reasoned, she already had a good idea of what the food was like, and Sandy's boyfriend, Manuel Lopez, could always help her out with firsthand details. It had seemed like a natural.

Jessica sat on the floor and began to flip through the magazine. How could she have forgotten? This was also the magazine in which she had first read about interpreting dreams. There had been the feature on Mexico, the article on dreams, and a very good piece on bath oils. She turned a few more pages and saw a photograph of Maui. Jessica stared at the picture in amazement. It was a full-color photograph of a beach on Maui. Her heart seemed to stop beating for a second. The beach looked disturbingly familiar. The sky was blue. The palm trees were swaying. And the sand was black. She leaned back against her bed. Had she seen *this* photograph and then dreamed about it? *Oh, don't be silly*, she scolded herself. *It's just a coincidence, that's what it is*. She turned a few more pages. Staring up at her from an ad for sportswear was a face that was more than familiar. Darkly handsome, smiling, and wearing a Hawaiian shirt. She was looking into the soft brown eyes of the boy of her dreams. Underneath him ran the caption *Jackson's Funtime Fashions—They Go Wherever You Go*. Jessica closed her eyes. "Oh, no," she said out loud, "tell me this isn't true." She opened her eyes. It was true. There was no getting away from it. And to make matters even worse, she had been so preoccupied with her Hawaiian fantasy that she hadn't bothered to get a real, live date for Saturday's dance.

Eleven

The Wakefield twins' little red Fiat Spider made its way toward Sweet Valley High. From inside, the sound of laughter floated into the chugging and beeping of morning traffic.

"Oh, you've got to be kidding, Jessica," Elizabeth roared. "The great love of your life turned out to be the model for Jackson's Funtime Fashions?"

"I don't think it's *that* funny, Elizabeth." Jessica frowned. "It was the sort of thing that could happen to anyone."

Elizabeth shook her head. Jessica always thought the messes she got into were no fault of her own. "Yeah," she said with a smile, "but it happened to you."

"Well, actually," Jessica went on, "if you want to know the truth, I think everything's happened for the best."

They stopped at a light, and Elizabeth turned to her sister with an awed expression on her face. "And exactly how do you figure that?"

119

Jessica smiled brightly, her usual enthusiasm beginning to bubble to the surface. "It's simple, Liz. I did so much reading on Hawaii when I was planning my trip, I don't really have too much more research to do for my English project. And Hawaii's much more interesting than Mexico. It's almost as if it were fated."

Elizabeth smiled. In a strange way, she had to admire Jessica. No matter what happened, her twin always bounced back stronger than ever.

Jessica tapped on the window frame with her bright pink nails. "The only thing that *hasn't* worked out is the fact that the biggest dance of the year is being held on Saturday night and I don't have a date for it!" She shook her head in wonder. "Talk about history in the making! Nothing like this has ever happened to me before!"

Elizabeth grimaced. "I'm not so sure that I've got one either," she admitted.

"Don't tell me you and Mr. Perfect have had a fight," Jessica said matter-of-factly.

Elizabeth swung the Fiat into the parking lot. "Not a fight, exactly," she explained. "But relations have been a little strained lately."

Jessica rolled her eyes. "It's because of that silly article you wrote, isn't it?"

They jerked to a stop. "Jessica," Elizabeth said in her calmest voice, "my article wasn't silly. In fact, it's raised a lot of important issues. It's gotten a very positive response from almost everyone."

"Not from me, it didn't," Jessica said as they climbed out of the car.

Elizabeth slammed her door shut. "It's all because of Scott Trost and his dumb contest," she explained. "Todd seems to think I've been too hard on Scott."

Jessica, seeing Amy and Cara up ahead, had started to hurry toward them, but at her sister's words she came to a stop. "Maybe that's what *I* should have done," she said thoughtfully.

"What is?" Elizabeth asked, wondering how they had gotten so quickly from talking about her to talking about Jessica.

"Why, entered Scott's contest, of course." Jessica flicked her hair over her shoulder. "Then at least I would have had a date for the dance."

"So, you've got your last date with Scott this afternoon, right?" Jean whispered. She and Claire had snuck into the girls' locker room together before classes began so they could have a final meeting.

Claire sat down on a bench. "And I can't wait." She sighed. "Two more hours of trying to think of something to say to Scott, and I'm a free woman."

Jean turned her attention to smoothing out her skirt. "I know what you mean," she said, not knowing what Claire meant at all. She never had any trouble finding things to say to Scott.

Claire shuddered. "No more of those awful five-minute silences, when all you can hear is the sound of us chewing or breathing. Ugh!"

"It certainly hasn't been any fun," Jean lied, thinking back to when they played miniature golf. She'd also had fun when they went for pizza. And she almost had fun the time she nearly set him on fire in the restaurant.

"All I want is for this whole ridiculous thing to be over with," Claire said. "Then I can get back to my real life." She smiled shyly. "And the boy I really like."

Jean came back to the locker room with a jolt. Her real life? The boy she really liked? What did Claire mean? A chill went through Jean as she realized the truth. Dating Scott *was* her real life. Being with him and looking forward to seeing him had become important to Jean. The memory of Scott trying for the twenty-fifth time to get his ball through the windmill at Golf City flashed before her eyes. She could hear his laughter. She could see his grin. Jean leaned against the lockers. How had she ever gotten herself into this mess? Scott Trost *was* the boy she really liked!

Elizabeth was sitting under a tree, waiting for Todd. She had suggested that they eat by themselves that day. She was hoping that a private lunch might clear some of the tension between them.

While she waited she reread the letter from Not Blind and Not Stupid. She had finally decided that Todd was right and that she should write a reply, but she wasn't quite sure where to start. As she stared at the typewritten lines, something began to nag at her. Elizabeth moved the letter into the light. What was it? It was just an ordinary typewritten letter. The author hadn't even signed it, but had typed out his pseudonym at the bottom. Elizabeth squinted. There was something very familiar about this letter, and it wasn't just that she had read it several times by now. *Oh, come on, Elizabeth,* she scolded herself, *it's typewritten. A typewriter is a typewriter. One typed letter is just like another.* She furrowed her brow and peered closer. But that was it! One typed letter *wasn't* just like another. Each typewriter was different. Her own typewriter had a slightly raised *r*. In this letter, the *a*'s were a little lopsided. Elizabeth bit her lip. Where had she seen that lopsided *a* before?

"Hi there!" called a cheerful voice. "How's my favorite blond?"

Elizabeth looked up to see Todd coming toward her, a big smile on his handsome face.

Automatically, she smiled back. "Hi yourself!" she replied. And then it came to her. The reason the letter she was holding looked so familiar was because she had seen that lopsided *a* a million times before. In homework assignments. In papers. In letters to her. She looked down at the paper in her hand and then back up at Todd. Not Blind and Not Stupid was none other than Todd Wilkins!

Todd leaned forward to give her a kiss but she shoved him back. "I don't believe this!" Elizabeth cried. She waved the letter in his face. "Todd Wilkins, you tried to trick me!"

But instead of apologizing, Todd plunked himself down beside her and started to laugh. "I really had you fooled, didn't I?" He grinned. "I was sure you'd know it was from me right away."

"Oh, were you?" Elizabeth asked coldly.

He nodded. "Absolutely."

"Then why did you write it?"

Todd put his arm around her shoulder. "Because you're so stubborn," he said affectionately. "And I couldn't get you to admit you were wrong."

"But I wasn't wrong!" Elizabeth declared.

"I know you weren't *completely* wrong," argued Todd. "But you yourself did say that I made some good points."

"And so did I," Elizabeth protested. She got to her feet.

"Now where are you going?" Todd asked. "I thought we were having lunch together."

Elizabeth picked up her things. "You'll have to excuse me," she said evenly. "I have a reply to write."

"What's the matter, Jean?" Sandy asked. Sandy had come over to Jean's house so they could do their history homework together, but Jean was showing no interest in what had happened in France two hundred years ago.

Jean shrugged and smiled at her friend. "I guess I'm just bored with all these dates."

Sandy winked. "That's probably because there's only one date you're really interested in at the moment."

For a minute Jean thought that Sandy was reading her mind. There was only one date that *was* interesting her at the moment, and it was taking place even as they spoke. Scott and Claire were on their last date. Jean had been thinking of nothing else all afternoon. At lunch she had seen Scott smile at Claire. It hadn't been an enormous smile, but it had been warm and friendly. And all at once it had occurred to Jean that just as she had given Claire edited versions of her dates with Scott, Claire could have been giving Jean edited versions as well. What if Claire really *didn't* find Scott tedious and boring? What if there really wasn't another boy that Claire had a crush on? Maybe she had only said that to throw Jean off the trail. Maybe Scott was the boy Claire really liked!

"Right, Jean?" Sandy repeated.

"What?"

"Not that I blame you," Sandy continued. "You must be really nervous. Tonight's your last date with him, isn't it?" She put down her pen. "Tomorrow's the big day, when Scott announces the winner!"

"That's right," Jean echoed. "Tomorrow's the big day."

"I guess you must be really excited," Sandy continued. "Tell me the truth, Jean," she said gently. "Do you think you're going to win?"

And what if Scott was playing games, too, Jean thought. More games, that was. What if he told Claire the same things he told her? That he meant everything that he'd said in his letter. That he wished he'd written only one letter, and that he'd written it to her. The tip of Jean's pencil snapped. She looked up to find Sandy staring at her.

"I can understand if you don't want to talk about it," Sandy said. "I mean, it must be making you crazy."

Jean laughed. Making her crazy! What an understatement! How crazy could she get, one minute worrying that Scott really didn't like her, and the next minute looking forward to making a fool out of him?

Sandy pushed her textbook out of the way, leaned over, and patted her friend's hand. "Don't worry, Jean. Claire doesn't have a chance against you."

"Oh, I'm not really worried," Jean said hurriedly.

"Are you sure?" Sandy asked. "Because I was thinking that after we finish our homework, we could plan what you're going to wear tonight. You really want to knock him dead, don't you?"

"Oh, I really want to knock him dead, all right." Jean laughed, but she didn't move her eyes from her book.

Sandy slid closer on the bed. "Look, Jean," she said. "I know Jessica and Lila think this contest is nothing but a lot of fun, but to tell you the truth, I'm not so sure. It seems pretty weird to me. If you don't want to go through with it, it's still not too late to tell Scott what a bum he is. Let him go to the dance by himself."

Jean knew that she couldn't keep the truth from Sandy any longer. She had to tell her at least *part* of it. Maybe not the part about her mixed feelings for Scott, but the part about the plan. "Well, as a matter of fact," she said flatly, "that's exactly the person Scott Trost is going to the dance with."

"Aren't you going to tell me where we're going?" Jean was sitting in the passenger seat, her eyes closed because Scott had "a big surprise" for her. She was only going along with him because talking to Sandy had made her feel so much better. For a little while, everything had seemed clear and straightforward: Scott was a total toad, and

Jean and Claire were in control. But sitting in the Corvette, driving for what seemed like hours, and listening to Scott talk and joke, things were beginning to seem less clear again. What was she doing, playing this game? "I'm taking my hands down," she announced. "I can't stand this any longer."

"No, don't!" Scott cried. "We're almost there, Jean. Don't ruin the surprise! Please." The car slowed down and pulled off the road. "You're going to like this, Jean, I know you are."

There was something so compelling in his voice that she found herself believing him.

"Now?" she asked impatiently.

"Not yet, not yet!" he cried. She could hear him bang into the car door in his hurry to get out. "Ow!" he muttered under his breath. And then, to her, "You can't look until you're out of the car."

"I'm not so sure about this," Jean said as he took her hands and helped her to her feet. They were at the beach. She could hear the roar of the ocean and feel the sand seeping into her shoes. "It's a little scary not being able to see," she said softly.

He put his arm around her shoulder. "You can trust me, Jean," he said in almost a whisper. "I wouldn't let anything happen to you."

Her heart turned over. She was beginning to forget that this was only a game.

Slowly, Scott led her across the sand. "OK," he said at last. "Open your eyes."

Jean blinked. She was staring into the most spectacular moonlit sky she'd ever seen. Stars cut the night like jewels and a full moon, tinged with orange, spilled light across the ocean and the sand.

"Well?" asked Scott. "What do you think?"

"Why, it's beautiful," Jean breathed. "It's the most beautiful thing I've ever seen."

Scott leaned his chin on her head and wrapped his arms around her waist. "I arranged it just for you," he whispered.

They walked in the moonlight. The farther they walked, the farther away the rest of the world seemed to be. The letters, the plan, the contest . . . everything that had seemed so important only a few hours before now seemed as far away as the smiling moon. For the first time since the whole thing had begun, Jean felt herself relax completely. She couldn't remember when she had felt this happy.

And when he took her in his arms this time, she didn't pull away. "It's always been you, Jean, right from the start." Scott put his lips to hers and kissed her. She had never been kissed like this before.

When she kissed him back, Jean wasn't pretending at all.

Twelve

Jean was late again Friday morning. She hadn't fallen into a really deep sleep until almost dawn. She was just getting her books from her locker when Claire came up behind her.

"What happened to you?" Claire asked in a low voice. "I was worried. I thought you were going to phone me and fill me in on your last date with Mr. Magic."

Jean slammed the door shut. "I'm sorry, Claire," she whispered back. "I was going to, I really was. But I was so tired by the time I got home that all I could do was crawl into bed."

"Having so much fun really takes it out of a girl, doesn't it?" Claire wisecracked. Then she looked more closely at Jean. "Gosh," she said, "you really do look tired."

Jean didn't know what to say. The reason she hadn't slept well the night before was because she had been worrying about what she should do about this stupid contest. Should she go through with the plan and make a fool out of Scott? Or should she tell Claire the truth, that her feelings for Scott had changed and that she wanted to call the whole thing off? Every time she decided to go through with their plan to humiliate Scott, she remembered the feeling of Scott's lips on hers and his arms around her. It made her feel as though her heart would break. Every time she decided to call it off, she remembered his arrogance and duplicity, and the only thing she wanted to break was his skull.

Jean managed a smile she wasn't feeling. "I guess all this pretending is more exhausting than I thought."

Claire winked. "Well, after lunchtime today, we won't have to pretend anymore," she said happily. "Once we have it out with Toad Trost, everything will go back to normal."

"Yeah," Jean agreed unenthusiastically, picturing those normal Saturday nights when she had to choose between watching television and teaching herself macramé. "What a relief."

Claire gave her a cheering smile. "Well, I just wanted to make sure you were all right." She glanced over her shoulder to where Jessica, Sandy, and Lila were standing in a line, staring at them. "I guess I'd better run before your friends get suspicious."

If she hadn't been feeling so depressed, Jean would have laughed. *Before Jessica and Lila got suspicious? If Jessica and Lila weren't teenagers, they would be FBI agents*, she thought. Claire hadn't taken more than one step away before Jessica and Lila rushed over, dragging Sandy behind them.

"What did she want?" asked Jessica, frowning after Claire's retreating back. "I bet she's getting nervous."

Lila sniffed. "She must realize she doesn't stand a chance against you. I mean, really—a girl who lets everybody see her in sweatpants and cleats thinking she can compete with a *cheerleader!*"

"What was she trying to do?" Jessica asked. "Psych you out?" She put an encouraging arm around Jean's shoulders. "Don't let her get to you, Jean. Just wait until Scott turns her down publicly." She beamed. "Then we'll all have a good laugh."

A good laugh? Jean's misery level soared. She was beginning to feel as though she might never laugh again. How had she ever gotten herself into this mess? She turned to Sandy for help.

"Jean," Sandy said softly, "don't you think you should tell them?"

"Tell us what?" asked Jessica and Lila together.

"It's about the contest . . ." Jean began.

Jessica and Lila moved closer, forming a small circle with Sandy and Jean.

"Don't tell me he's already picked Claire!" Lila asked in an outraged whisper. "Is he out of his mind?"

"Don't tell me the whole thing's off!" Jessica grumbled. "I had a hunch this would happen. Just last night I had this dream—"

Lila glared at her. "Please, Jessica, we've all had enough of your dreams."

"You're both wrong," Jean cut in quickly. She glanced to Sandy, who smiled in support. "Maybe I'd better start at the beginning."

There was a moment of stunned silence after

131

Jean had finished her story about the identical love letters. Then Jessica stamped her foot. "Why, that creep!" she hissed. "Who does he think he is?"

"He's nobody. That's who he is," Lila said sharply. "And nobody is exactly what he's going to feel like when he finds out the truth!"

"Don't you worry, Jean," Jessica reassured her. "We'll make sure he learns his lesson."

Jean smiled weakly. "That's terrific. I can't wait."

Jean sat numbly through first period. All she could think of was what awaited her at the end of her morning classes. Contrary to what Jean had told her friends, she could happily have waited forever for lunchtime and the moment of truth to arrive. She only knew that history class was over when everyone else got up to leave.

Still half in a daze, Jean was on her way to her next class when she bumped into Elizabeth.

Elizabeth gave her a wink. "It won't be long now," she said.

Jean stared at her blankly.

Elizabeth looked around to make sure no one else was within hearing distance. "It's all right, Jean," she said softly. "I know all about your plan." Seeing that Jean's bewildered expression didn't immediately change to one of understanding, she rushed on. "I hope you don't mind that Claire told me, but I sort of forced it out of her." Elizabeth put her hand on her heart. "But I haven't told a soul," she promised.

"Oh, right," Jean mumbled. "Sure, that's fine."

"I guess you must be pretty excited," Elizabeth continued. Her smile was warm and kind. "After pretending for so long, at last you get to tell Scott the truth."

Jean started to say, "Yes, of course, I'm really excited," but something in the sympathetic way Elizabeth was looking at her made the words die in her throat. Instead of telling another fib, she burst into tears.

Elizabeth immediately put a hand on her shoulder. "Jean," she said gently. "Jean, what's wrong?"

"Oh, Elizabeth," Jean choked, trying to control her sobs. "I've made such a mess of everything. I just don't know what to do."

There was an empty classroom behind them, and without a second's hesitation Elizabeth took hold of Jean and pulled her inside. "Now tell me what's wrong," she said once the door was safely shut behind them. She took a tissue out of her bag and handed it to Jean. "From what Claire said, I'd say it's Scott who made a mess of everything. All you've done is make it possible for you and Claire to get your revenge against him after he treated you both so badly."

Jean wiped her tears with Elizabeth's tissue. "Oh, Elizabeth," she whispered, "that's just the trouble. I don't think I want to get my revenge any longer."

"What do you mean?"

Jean stared miserably at the sopping tissue in her hand. "I mean, I think I've fallen in love with Scott!"

"Did I hear you right?" Elizabeth asked as gently as she could. "Did you say you're in love with Scott?"

Jean nodded, slowly raising her face to Elizabeth's. "That's what I said." She smiled, though her eyes were still sparkling with tears. "I don't know how it happened, Elizabeth. I was so mad at him when I found out what he'd done, asking both me and Claire out. And then when he was so arrogant in the cafeteria, I don't think I've ever disliked anyone so much in my life." She started to cry again.

Elizabeth handed her the entire packet of tissues. "Well, something must have happened to make you go from total dislike to love. I'll admit, Scott's not my favorite person, but Todd thinks he's OK. And now if *you* like him . . ."

Jean laughed through her tears. "I know it's hard to believe," she said, "but it's *him*." She shrugged helplessly. "Oh, I don't even know what I'm trying to say, Elizabeth. It's just that we really seemed to get along. We really seemed to like each other a lot. And now I don't know what to do or what to think."

"Jean," Elizabeth asked softly, "have you told Claire what you just told me?"

Jean shook her head. "I almost said something this morning, but I was so confused . . ."

Jean's confusion made Elizabeth feel surer of her own judgment. She decided to take charge. "Well, that's what you've got to do, then, Jean," she advised her. "You can't possibly go through with your original plan feeling the way you do. You've *got* to call the whole thing off before it's too late!"

But by the time Jean finally caught up with Claire as she was hurrying to the lunchroom, she was beginning to realize that some things are more easily said than done.

"Claire," Jean hissed, catching hold of her sleeve. "Claire, I've got to talk to you."

Claire stopped and turned. Her eyes were bright with excitement. "What is it, Jean?" she whispered back.

"I just need to have a quick word with you before we confront Scott."

Claire's look of excitement turned to one of surprise. "Now?" she asked. "You must be kidding. Everyone's waiting for us, Jean."

"They'll wait another minute or two," Jean said desperately. "It won't take long, Claire, and it's really important."

"What's wrong, Jean? Are you nervous? Because if you are, I don't mind doing most of the talking." Claire shook her fist in the air. "I've been waiting a long time to tell Scott exactly what I think of him."

Jean suddenly realized that they were walking again and that the doors to the cafeteria were straight ahead of them, as welcoming as the gates of hell. "No, it's not that, Claire," Jean said. "It's something else."

Claire sailed through the doors and into the cafeteria, Jean two steps behind her and trying to pull her to a stop.

"I think this is going to have to wait, Jean. I really have to—" Claire broke off in the middle of her sentence. Then she said, "Oh, my gosh, I feel like I'm in the middle of the field during a big game."

Jean now looked around. "I don't believe this,"

she breathed. Claire was right: every eye in the room was focused on them. Claire hadn't been kidding when she said everyone had been waiting for them. Everyone was. Jean turned her eyes to her friends. Jessica, Amy, and Sandy were all smiling at her.

And then the door on the other side of the cafeteria opened, and in walked Scott. Every head turned in his direction. But for a second he didn't notice. He stood in the entrance, his eyes on Jean, a soft smile on his lips. Her heart turned over. But then she saw him take in the staring eyes, and his smile set. He raised his head, stood up taller, and started striding toward the center of the room.

Very lightly, Claire reached backward and brushed her hand against Jean's. "This is it," she whispered. "Let's go!"

Jean counted every step as she and Claire crossed the room. It felt as though she were walking over hot coals. She had to do something to get out of this awful mess, and she had to do it fast. Why hadn't she told Claire the truth when she had the opportunity? Why had she let it go this far? She knew that Scott was watching them, smiling like a game-show host, but she kept her eyes on a point above his head.

They came to a stop a few feet from where Scott had casually seated himself on top of a table.

"So, Prince Charming," Winston Egbert shouted out, "which of these fair damsels is it to be?"

There was a chorus of laughter from some of the boys, and then an awkward silence descended on the cafeteria.

Now, Jean urged herself. *Before this goes an inch further, call the whole thing off!*

Jean took a deep breath and cleared her throat. It wasn't going to be easy, but it had to be done. She cleared her throat one last time. A strong, confident voice filled the room. Unfortunately, though, the strong, confident voice wasn't Jean's. The voice belonged to Scott.

"This has been a very difficult choice to make," the voice said.

But it wasn't the voice she'd become used to over the past week, the voice that had made her laugh, the voice that had whispered to her so passionately on the beach the previous night. This was the patronizing, condescending voice of Scott Trost the arrogant superjock. This was the voice of the boy who had said that anything worth having was worth fighting for and had set himself up as a prize.

"Both Claire and Jean are great girls," the voice continued. "And I'm sure going to miss having the two of them fighting over me."

From somewhere nearby, Jean heard one boy whisper to another, "Can you beat it? This guy thinks he's a rock star or something."

All the confusion and anguish of the last few days vanished. It was as though a heavy curtain had been lifted from over her head. Suddenly, everything was clear. She had been right from the start. Scott Trost had no redeeming qualities. How could she have been such a fool, she wondered. This wasn't a sensitive and warm human being. This was an egomaniac who had selfishly put her and Claire in a demeaning position.

"But I'm a man of my word," the voice said. "I promised I'd come to a decision by today, and I have."

Jean looked over to where her friends were standing, their eyes on her. She could imagine what Lila would say if she knew that Jean had actually thought she was in love with Scott. *You should get out more, Jean,* Lila would say. *That way you wouldn't have to scrape the bottom of the barrel.* She looked back to Scott. This was a smug, conceited chauvinist who believed that any girl should be grateful for his attention. And she had fallen for him. She had been less than honest with Claire. She had singlehandedly set the women's movement back eighty years. Jean wished the ground would open up and swallow her whole. She had never felt so humiliated in all her life.

Scott was holding out his hand. "My date for tomorrow night's dance is Jean West," he announced grandly.

But not everyone heard him, because Jean had begun to shout. "I wouldn't go out with you if you were the last boy on earth!" she screamed, her face red with fury. She could see the shock and surprise on his face, and it made her even angrier. "And if you *were* the last boy on earth," she continued, "you'd better believe I'd demand a recount!" From the table beside her she grabbed what she hoped was a full container of milk and threw it in Scott's direction before she ran from the room in a flood of tears. The cafeteria door banged shut behind Jean and all eyes returned to Scott.

Claire was aware of the ripple of embarrassment that passed through the room. Even Winston couldn't think of anything to say.

Claire was also aware that Scott had recovered enough of his composure to be grinning again. "Well," he said, his bravado returning, "I guess

some people aren't cut out for real competition."
He gave a nervous little laugh. "You know what
they say. If you can't stand the heat . . ." He
turned to Claire. "I guess you're the lucky winner
after all."

Claire gave a short laugh. "Don't do me any
favors." She smiled at him, completely in control.
"I just want you to know that everything that Jean
said goes double for me."

Suddenly, Danny Porter stepped forward and
put an arm around Claire's shoulders. He looked
Scott in the eye. "They're both too good for you,
if you want my opinion," he said.

"Well, I don't want your opinion," Scott sneered.
"I wouldn't be surprised if you had set this whole
thing up from the beginning." He took a step
toward Danny. "That's it, isn't it, Porter? This is
all your doing."

"Don't blame Danny, Scott," Claire said. "The
only enemy you've got is yourself." And with that
she slipped her arm around Danny and the two
of them walked from the room, leaving Scott
standing alone in the middle of the cafeteria.

"Hey, Trost!" someone shouted from the back
of the room. "Don't bother saving the last dance
for me, OK?"

Elizabeth raced after Claire and Danny.
"Claire!" she called. "Claire! What happened?
What went wrong?"

Claire was leaning against Danny and laughing
in earnest now. "Nothing went wrong, Liz," she
said in surprise. "Everything went exactly
according to plan." Her smile was radiant. "I told
Danny I'd go to the dance with him days ago,
and Jean and I accomplished what we set out to

do. We showed Scott up for the awful person he is."

Elizabeth stared at her in disbelief. "You mean, Jean didn't tell you?"

Instantly, Claire's expression became serious. "Tell me what?"

"So then what did Claire say?" Jessica asked. The twins were sitting on Elizabeth's bed, going over the amazing events of the day. Elizabeth had been telling Jessica what had happened after she followed Claire from the cafeteria.

"Well, she was completely astounded, of course. She didn't have any idea that Jean was getting serious about Scott."

Jessica twisted another bright rubber rod into her hair. "Sandy and I looked all over for Jean, but she never showed up for any of her afternoon classes."

Elizabeth shook her head. "I tried calling her this afternoon, but she wouldn't speak to me." She handed her sister another curler. "Claire and I are going to go over there tomorrow and try to talk to her. Can you imagine how she must feel?"

Jessica held the hand mirror up to her face. "I think you're exaggerating as usual, Liz," Jessica said. "I'm sure Jean's fine. She didn't say anything to me about having a crush on Scott." She adjusted a purple curler. "And anyway, it doesn't pay to meddle in other people's lives," she said sagely. "You should have learned that by now."

"Oh, right, Jessica." Elizabeth nodded. "In the future, I'll try to follow your sterling example."

Thirteen

"I don't suppose there's any chance you and Todd aren't going to the dance tonight?" Jessica asked as Elizabeth pulled the Fiat to a stop in front of the library.

"As far as I know we're going," Elizabeth replied. She tried to keep the little bit of doubt she was feeling out of her voice, but the truth was that she hadn't really spoken to Todd since she had snapped at him for tricking her. She knew that if he had seen her reply to his letter in *The Oracle*, he'd know that she was sorry. But she wasn't sure if he had seen it. "With all the craziness yesterday, I didn't really get a chance to speak to him, and last night he had to go somewhere with his parents. Why?"

Jessica shrugged. "I just thought that if you weren't busy, we could do something together."

A look of surprise came over Elizabeth's face. As much as the twins loved each other, it wasn't every day that Jessica showed any interest in

141

socializing with her sister. "Why, Jessica," Elizabeth said, "that's really sweet of you."

"Well, I have to do something tonight, don't I?" Jessica pouted. "Since I don't have a date."

"Oh, right." Elizabeth laughed. "I should have known it wasn't because you wanted my company."

Jessica gathered her things from the back seat. "It's not that, Liz," she said. "It's just that I don't know what people who don't go out *do* on Saturday nights. Are there special shows on television for them, or something like that?"

"Oh, I'm sure there are," Elizabeth said mischievously. "Sing-alongs and things like that." She watched as Jessica adjusted the stack of books she was returning. "Are you sure you can manage all by yourself?" she asked. "I can give you a hand if you want."

"It's OK, Liz," Jessica said. "I think I can handle it. At least if I strain my back, I can spend the evening with a heating pad."

Elizabeth got out and went around to the other side to open her sister's door. "Do you want me to pick you up on my way home, after I've seen Jean?"

Jessica shook her head. "No. I've got to put a couple of finishing touches on my English project, so I'm not sure how long I'll be." She leaned against the side of the car. "If I'm lucky, maybe it'll take me all night."

Elizabeth patted her shoulder. "Try not to suffer too much, OK? You'll get frown lines." She got back into the Fiat. "I'll see you later," she called.

"Maybe." Jessica sighed dramatically.

*   *   *

On their way to Jean's house, Elizabeth and Claire discussed how they were going to approach Jean.

"She didn't sound too keen about seeing us when I talked to her on the phone," Claire admitted. "I practically had to tell her mother it was a matter of life and death before she'd even speak to me."

"I can understand how upset she must be," Elizabeth said, "but I'm also sure that she needs to talk to someone about it. Whether or not she decides to give Scott another chance, she can't keep her feelings bottled up inside."

Claire nodded. "If only I'd known what was happening, I would have put a stop to it."

"Well, that doesn't matter now," Elizabeth said philosophically. "What matters is Jean. We've got to try to convince her to at least talk to Scott, so she can straighten everything out in her own mind."

Elizabeth parked the car in front of the Wests' house. Side by side, she and Claire marched up the concrete pathway.

"I hope she isn't taking it *too* hard," Elizabeth said as they neared the porch.

"She's very sensitive," Claire answered. "I'm sure this isn't easy for her."

They exchanged a worried look as they came to a stop before the front door. "She's probably been crying her eyes out all night long," Claire whispered as Elizabeth rang the bell.

"I know," Elizabeth whispered back. "Poor kid. She probably can't eat or sleep, either."

Both of them were expecting that the door would open to reveal a pale, gaunt figure with a box of tissues in her hand who would take a look at them and immediately burst into tears.

But when the door swung open, there before them was a bright-eyed and smiling Jean who looked as healthy and well-fed as she always did. Instead of beginning to sob, the first words out of Jean's mouth were, "It's no use. I don't even want to hear his name."

"Whose name?" Elizabeth teased, slightly taken aback.

"You know whose," Jean answered. She scowled. *"His."*

"Um, Jean," Claire said gently, "do you mind if we come in?"

Jean seemed surprised to discover that she was blocking the entranceway. "Oh, no, of course not," she said quickly. And just as quickly added, "But I don't want you to think that I'm going to change my mind."

Well, Elizabeth thought, *I guess we didn't have to worry about Jean pining away from a broken heart after all.*

"Change your mind about what?" Elizabeth asked innocently.

Jean studied them closely. "You've come to convince me to change my mind about Scott, haven't you?"

"Of course we haven't, Jean," Claire assured her. "I'd be the last person to do that."

"Well, I'm certainly glad to hear it." Jean smiled. "The only reason I didn't want to talk to you on the phone was because I was afraid you wanted to discuss you-know-who." She led them

144

into the living room. "As far as I'm concerned," she said firmly, "the matter is completely closed. I plan to get on with my life as though none of it ever happened."

Claire glanced at Elizabeth. Elizabeth shrugged. It certainly didn't look as though Jean needed their help.

"Can I get you a soda or something?" Jean asked, turning to face them. "Please," she said, "sit down."

Claire and Elizabeth sat on the couch together and Jean sat across from them.

"Oh, no," said Elizabeth, "we can't stay long." She glanced uneasily at Claire. She had had her speech to Jean pretty well mapped out, but now she was at a loss for words. Contrary to what she and Claire had imagined, Jean apparently was coping with a vengeance. Elizabeth's smile brightened. Impossible as it seemed, it looked like Jessica had been right!

"We just wanted to see how you were," Claire said. "We were a little worried about you."

"No need to worry about me," Jean said brightly. "I'm fine."

"Well, you certainly look fine," Claire agreed.

"And I feel fine, too," Jean affirmed. "I'm a new woman!"

But Elizabeth *couldn't* believe that Jessica was right. When she had spoken to Jean the day before, Jean had been both very upset and very much in love. It wasn't unusual for Elizabeth's twin to fall in and out of love in the course of an afternoon, but Elizabeth couldn't believe that Jean was like that. It had taken her a long time to get over Tom McKay. Elizabeth made up her mind.

She was going to say what she had come to say. "Jean," she said gently. "I was wondering . . . don't you think that maybe you should talk to Scott?"

"Scott?" Jean asked politely. "I'm sorry, I don't think I know anyone by that name."

Claire tried to intercede. "But Jean," she began. "Elizabeth and I just thought that—"

Jean got to her feet. "Elizabeth, Claire, I appreciate your concern, but as you can see, you're wasting your time." She folded her arms across her chest and met their eyes. "As far as I'm concerned, I've done all the talking to Scott Trost I'm ever going to do in my life. I mean, really. Talk about consorting with the enemy! I not only handed him my gun, I practically pulled the trigger for him!"

"But, Jean, yesterday you said—"

Jean held up her hands. "I don't care what I said yesterday, Elizabeth. Yesterday I was wrong."

"We just thought that if there was something about Scott that made you feel . . . made you think that . . ." The look in Jean's eyes made it difficult for Claire to continue.

"Why don't you just come right out and say it?" Jean asked in a flat, calm voice. "Love. I thought I was in love with him!" She started to laugh. "Can you believe it? Am I the biggest fool you've ever known, or what?"

Elizabeth stood up. "Jean, we don't think you're a fool. We just think that if you found something in Scott to love, then maybe it's worth at least hearing what he has to say."

"Well, I don't," Jean said simply. "I appreciate

your coming over here," she told them as she walked them to the door. "But I really don't want to discuss this anymore."

When the girls had said their goodbyes, Jean shut the door behind Claire and Elizabeth and heaved a sigh of relief. She'd done it! Not only had she convinced them that she was all right, she'd convinced them that she was totally over Scott. *Really, Jean,* she congratulated herself, *you should join the drama club.*

As soon as Jean heard Elizabeth's car drive away, she went back into the living room and threw herself on the couch. She reached under one of the cushions and removed the wad of tissues she had hidden there. She lay on her back and stared at the ceiling.

She couldn't sleep. Every time she closed her eyes she saw Scott's face. Sometimes it was the face that had whispered words of love to her on Thursday night. And sometimes it was the face that had challenged her and Claire to a contest over him. Both of them were driving her crazy.

She couldn't eat. Almost every date she'd had with Scott had involved eating. But just the thought of him made the food in her mouth taste like dust. She would probably never be able to touch pizza again. Especially not with mushrooms.

She moaned out loud. For the four-millionth time she asked herself, "How?" How could the sweet, sensitive, funny boy she had fallen in love with share a body with the arrogant creep she loathed? Was it a case of Quarterback Trost and Mr. Hyde?

How could she have collected so many memories in so short a period of time? The miniature-golf game. The fancy restaurant. Moonlight on the beach.

She was just wiping the newest tears from her eyes when the doorbell rang. She popped up so quickly she nearly fell off the couch. Panicking, she looked around the room. There, near her feet, was Claire's shoulder bag. She must have realized she'd left it behind and come back for it. Quickly, she dried her eyes, straightened her skirt, and patted her hair back into shape. The doorbell rang again, a little more insistently this time.

"I'm coming!" she called.

She picked up the bag and hurried to the hall. She put a big smile on her face. "Here it is!" she cried as she threw open the door. "I just this minute noticed—"

Jean's heart banged to a halt. Instead of Claire's brown eyes, she was staring into the dark blue ones of Scott.

"Jean!" he said in a rush. "Jean, I've got to talk to you!"

She grabbed for the heavy wooden door.

"Don't shut it," he pleaded. He threw his weight against it and wedged his foot between the door and the frame. "I'm begging you, Jean. Just give me a chance to explain."

The only reason she didn't scream at him was because suddenly she was incapable of speech. The last thing she'd expected was a visit from him. He wasn't the type to apologize. The Scott Trost of the previous day's confrontation was not the sort of guy to come begging for forgiveness. Nor was the Scott Trost of the two love letters and the childish contest the type to lose sleep over

148

a girl. But though she was trying hard not to look at him, she could see the dark circles under his eyes. *Oh, no,* she thought, *it's happening again!*

"Jean," he implored her. "Please. All I'm asking for is five minutes of your time. Five minutes and then if you never want to see me again, you never will."

Warning bells were going off in her head. *Don't do it,* said a tiny voice above all the noise of the bells. *Don't fall for his lines again.*

"Jean, I know I've behaved like the biggest creep the world has ever seen, and I know there's no way of making up to you for that, but please, Jean, just give me five minutes to explain."

I know his type, said the voice. *Give him five minutes and he'll be here for the next three hours.*

He sounded so sincere. She stepped back.

A second voice joined the first. *He really is different,* it said. *This is the boy I love.*

Can't you see this is Quarterback Trost? said the first voice. *Any minute now he's going to turn back into Mr. Hyde!*

Five minutes, said the second voice. *That's not too much to ask!*

You're going to regret this, warned the first voice.

Jean took another step back. "There isn't any explanation for your behavior," she told him coolly. "You treated Claire and me as though we were dolls."

He moved into the hall. "I know I did, Jean, and I'm going to apologize to Claire, too. I don't know what happened. But the other guys were kidding me about being dumped all the time and not being able to get a date . . ."

She stared at his shoes. "So you thought you'd

149

make sure you got a date." She looked up at him and her eyes were blazing. "I'm surprised you stopped at two letters, Scott. Why didn't you send ten or twelve?"

He moved toward her. "I just wanted a little backup, Jean. I—"

She took another step back. "I don't want to hear any more of your lies, Scott."

"Jean, please, I'm not lying. I don't know, it's as if I'm two people. There's the outside me, the big-mouthed jock, and then there's the inside me, the person I'd really like to be." His voice became soft and his words came slowly. "The inside me is the person I was when you and I were alone, Jean. You're the first girl I've ever felt comfortable with."

She backed into the wall. "I don't understand," she said flatly. "If that's the person you want to be, then why don't you just be him and stop acting like such a creep?"

He seemed genuinely bewildered. "I don't know. I really don't know. Sometimes I think it's because I think that the guys expect me to act a certain way. And sometimes I think it's because girls expect me to."

"Oh, come on," Jean said sharply. "Give me a break."

"Not you, Jean, and not Claire. But other girls. Really. They think if you don't act like a big man, you must be weak."

She started to protest, but he rushed ahead.

"I know it's dumb, Jean, but whenever I start to relax and act like my real self—I don't know what it is, I just seem to panic. I start imagining that everybody's going to think I'm soft or something."

She tried to slide to the right but bumped into the hat stand. "But that sweet, kind you is the you I fell in love with," she whispered.

"And he's the one who fell in love with you, Jean," he whispered back.

She had to put her hands on his chest to keep herself from melting into his arms. "I'm not saying I will, but if I do forgive you, Scott, you have to understand that you're on probation. If you do one tiny little thing that's arrogant or mean, it's all over between us and I really will never speak to you again."

He took hold of her wrists and pulled her arms around him. "I wouldn't have it any other way," he said softly, bringing his lips to hers.

And then, because there was nothing more to say, she kissed him.

After she dropped Claire off, Elizabeth drove into town to do some errands for her mother. She stopped at the bakery and picked up a loaf of French bread. She went to the pet store for flea powder for Prince Albert. The last stop was the drugstore. She was choosing a shampoo when she heard a familiar voice behind her. "After yesterday, I think I'd rather be an aardvark than a teenage boy," it said.

Elizabeth felt a rush of joy run through her. She knew without looking that Todd was behind her. "I don't think I'd like you as much if you were an aardvark." She laughed, turning around.

"And if I were an aardvark, I wouldn't have been able to read your great reply to my letter." Todd smiled and took her hands in his. "Does this mean I still have a date for the dance?"

Elizabeth laughed. "It'll be a disappointment to my sister." She smiled. "But you definitely have a date, Mr. Wilkins." She kissed his cheek. "Just try to get out of it."

Mrs. Wakefield was sitting in the living room reading when the front door suddenly banged open. She looked up just in time to see Jessica racing up the stairs.

"Jessica!" she called. "What's the hurry?"

Jessica spun around. Her face was flushed and her eyes were sparkling like the ocean on a sunny day. "I can't stop to chat now, Mom. I've got to get ready for the dance!"

Mrs. Wakefield gazed at her daughter for a second. "I thought you weren't going to the dance," she said. "I thought your life was in ruins and you would probably never have another date as long as you lived."

"Oh, Mom." Jessica sighed impatiently. "Of course I'm going to the dance. I'm going with Steve Anderson. He was in the library, and when I just happened to drop all my books at his feet he helped me pick them up." She gave her mother a big smile. "You know how it is, Mom. One thing naturally led to another."

Mrs. Wakefield smiled, too. "Oh, yes," she said, "I think I've lived with you long enough to know exactly how it is."

*   *   *

It was the perfect evening for the perfect dance. The gym was decorated in a riot of paper flowers, paper hearts, and silver balloons. Outside, candles flickered in the dark, and inside a pale stream of moonlight washed through the windows.

Jessica floated across the dance floor in Steve Anderson's strong arms. Now that she was so close to him, she could see how much he resembled the boy in her dreams. She sighed contentedly. *Who was it who said, "All's well that ends well?"* she wondered. Not far away she could see Elizabeth and Todd, dancing dreamily together, and, near them, Claire with Danny and Jean with Scott. It would have been hard to award a prize to the happiest-looking couple, Jessica thought, that was for sure. She smiled to herself.

"What's so funny?" Steve asked.

Jessica laughed. "Oh, I was just thinking about how dreams really can come true," she replied.

Steve smiled back. "They certainly can."

Across the dance floor, Sara Eastborne danced in the arms of her boyfriend, senior Bob Hillman. Sara had been at Sweet Valley High only since the beginning of the school year, but already she was well liked. She had made a best friend in Amanda Hayes, and had begun to date Bob soon after.

"Happy?" Bob asked as he pulled Sara closer to him.

"Umm," Sara replied, closing her eyes and leaning her head on his shoulder. It was true, Sara was happy. Happier than she had ever been, now that she and her mother were safely settled in Sweet Valley, far away from the troubles that had caused her family to fall apart. Suddenly, Sara felt herself shiver lightly as a memory of those terrible times crossed her mind.

"Are you cold?" Bob murmured in her ear.

"No. I'm fine," Sara assured him. No matter what, she would not let the past interfere with the present, not now that she had what she'd worked so hard to have—a stable life. Only one person could disturb her new-found happiness, and that person was far away. That person was her twin brother, Tim. As far as anyone at Sweet Valley High knew, Tim had stayed on the east coast with their father when the Eastbornes had divorced. And that's all anyone had to know.

Sara pulled a bit away from Bob and smiled up at him. "You're great, you know that?"

Bob smiled back and once again wrapped her in his strong, protective embrace.

Can Sara's hard-won happiness last? Find out in Sweet Valley High #79, **THE LONG LOST BROTHER.**